"Two can play at that game," Laura whispered provocatively

"What are you doing?" Clint murmured, aware that their suspects were watching them on the dance floor.

"Why, playing the part of the loving wife," Laura purred. She raised herself up on her toes to brush a kiss along the side of Clint's mouth, pleased to feel his arms tighten around her, to see his dark eyes filled with raw need.

Unaware that the music had stopped, she pulled his head to her and pressed her lips ravenously over his. Clint's hands curved over her hips in primal exploration, squeezing gently and sending liquid heat through her body. Her heart pounded in her ears until she realized it wasn't rushing blood she was hearing.

Applause from the restaurant patrons jolted them back to reality like a bucket of cold water. Laura quickly turned her shocked expression into a smile. She couldn't let Clint know that her kisses had been anything more than part of their assignment.

"I think we've made our point," she said, turning on her heel. "Although I must admit, if I'd known that cowboys kissed so well, I'd have visited Texas long ago."

Dear Reader,

I'm convinced I adore cowboys because watching them on television taught me how to speak English. Although I was born in Toronto, Canada, my parents were from Estonia and I grew up speaking Estonian. I learned English by playing with all my friends who spoke Greek, Italian and an assortment of other languages (Toronto is very multicultural) and by watching TV with my dad—hence my second passion for television.

My father preferred Westerns, and I spent many an hour watching these shows, falling in love with the rugged, do-the-right-thing, let-nothing-stand-in-his-way cowboy. Whether he's the strong silent type or a silver-tongued charmer, the cowboy is my perfect romantic hero.

Which made writing about Clint Marshall and Two Mule Junction such fun. Pairing him with his complete opposite, a Boston blue blood with a silly dog, only made the possibilities entertainingly unending. I hope you enjoy *A Stetson on Her Pillow* as much as I did.

Happy trails!

Molly Liholm

Books by Molly Liholm

HARLEQUIN TEMPTATION
552—TEMPTING JAKE
643—BOARDROOM BABY
672—THE GETAWAY GROOM
706—THE ADVENTUROUS BRIDE
745—BABY.COM

A STETSON ON HER PILLOW
Molly Liholm

HARLEQUIN®

TORONTO • NEW YORK • LONDON
AMSTERDAM • PARIS • SYDNEY • HAMBURG
STOCKHOLM • ATHENS • TOKYO • MILAN • MADRID
PRAGUE • WARSAW • BUDAPEST • AUCKLAND

For Nancy Hill, superachiever, who is always looking
for new challenges and adventures.

ISBN 0-373-25962-X

A STETSON ON HER PILLOW

Copyright © 2002 by Malle Vallik.

This edition published by arrangement with Harlequin Books S.A.

® and TM are trademarks of the publisher. Trademarks indicated with
® are registered in the United States Patent and Trademark Office, the
Canadian Trade Marks Office and in other countries.

Visit us at www.eHarlequin.com

Printed in U.S.A.

1

"YOU WANT ME to marry the cowboy?" Laura asked. "You expect *me*," she punctuated the word with a tone of disbelief, "to marry *him?*"

Even as she spoke in her low, cultured voice and brushed a strand of blond hair off her face, securing it back into the neat French braid she favored, Clint Marshall knew their boss had already made up his mind. They had been called into his office to receive their marching orders—not to debate whether or not they wanted the assignment.

Still, he found it downright amusing to watch patrician Laura Carter try to wiggle her skinny behind out of the assignment. Her cold-blue eyes, a color that reminded Clint of the silver blue of a Texas sky just before a storm, swept over him, quickly dismissed him and returned to Captain Clark.

Clint slouched farther down on the hard wooden chair and crossed one well-worn cowboy boot over the other. He felt Laura's gaze fall on the scuffed leather. He swung the foot back and forth as if he were relaxing on a rocking chair on his mother's porch and wished he had a cowboy hat he could tilt forward and drive little Miss Prim and Proper plum crazy. Not that she showed it, but he knew his good old boy routine had gotten to her as she sat even straighter in her chair. Not for the first time he wondered what a Boston blue blood was doing on the Chicago police force.

Or why in the world their captain would be assigning the two of them to work together.

Undoubtedly the skinny, pale man standing in the corner of the office had something to do with this. From the stranger's expensive, but ill-fitting, suit and polished shoes Clint knew he wasn't a regular cop. He didn't look like a guy who knew what the inside of a patrol car looked like much less smelled like. He reminded Clint of an accountant.

In fact he reminded Clint of Jason Fairmount, a nervous tweedy fellow who arrived in Two Horse Junction twice a year to offer his accountancy services. Clint's mother always had Jason over for dinner whenever he was in town, saying she admired him, and that she wished one of her sons could be as responsible and reliable as Jason.

The skinny, pale man wiped his brow and waited for Captain Clark to speak. Clint kept his mouth shut. There was no point in asking why he and the ice princess had been chosen for this confidential assignment. Captain Clark would tell them when he was ready. If there was one thing Clint knew how to do, it was how to wait.

Instead he smiled at Laura and settled back in his chair, still pretending that it was a comfortable rocker and not a bare-boned, hard-assed flimsy excuse for a chair. Why, such a chair wouldn't even last through one fight at the Two Horse Watering Hole back home.

Laura glanced at the stranger who was standing silently behind them, opened her mouth, but then closed it again without a word of protest. Clint knew she was annoyed at being assigned to work a case with him. For some reason, Laura Carter had taken one look at him six months ago and decided she didn't like him.

Of course, he didn't like her much better.

But if successfully completing this assignment meant that he had a chance to move up to the vacant detective position in Homicide he would work with anyone—including Laura Carter.

He wondered if the rumors about her were true. She had transferred into their unit six months ago after an alleged affair with her boss. Her new boss, Sam Clark, hated having the brass chose his officers for him. Anytime the captain had joined the team for drinks Clint had heard him say that the reason his unit had such a good arrest record was because he chose his detectives without political interference.

Until Laura Carter.

Clark had given her all the crappy assignments, like looking for bond jumpers and investigating small-scale burglaries and purse snatchings. When she'd caught a burglar who'd been stealing from local businesses for over a year, Clark had grudgingly commended her on a job well done.

Laura took a deep breath, looking like a particularly ornery mule about to set out on its own path, ignoring the fact that it would never find its way back home. Clint decided to rescue her before she made another mistake and complained about the assignment further—especially the part about being married to him.

"Darlin', most of the single women on Chicago's finest would jump at the chance to be Mrs. Clint Marshall. If there's one thing us Texas men are known for, it's for treating a woman right."

She stiffened even more. He wondered if any man ever got her to loosen up enough to uncross her gorgeous legs and... Well, he wouldn't let his thoughts continue on their ungentlemanly path. No matter what Ms. Laura Carter thought about his manners, his mother had raised him right.

He let his lips quirk in a half smile as Laura studied him coldly. Her porcelain skin turned even whiter as a slash of pink burned along her high cheekbones. "First, no matter how foolishly some of the other women in this department behave, I'm not part of your female fan club," she said. "Second, I wouldn't identify myself by my husband's name even if he was a Nobel Prize winner for establishing world peace and finding a safe, nonpolluting, inexpensive form of energy." She tightened her lips in a thin line as she contemplated the unappealing prospect of being married to him. "*Mrs. Clint Marshall.* That is so outdated and macho! Finally, the last thing I would ever want from you would be to be treated *just right.*"

She thrust out her chin and glared at him, sparks sizzling from those blue eyes. For the first time Clint saw that there was a tiny ember of fire in her. What could be more fun than to make it burn higher—to make the rigid, frigid Laura Carter burn with anger—and then maybe something else? He wondered what she would be like in bed, with those long, slim legs wrapped around a man, her hair loose and wild about her face. Startled out of his unexpected fantasy about Laura, he winked at her. "Trust me darlin', if you don't want it, then you've never been treated *just right.*" He drawled the last two words in his best Texas twang.

"Stop calling me darling," she said between gritted teeth.

Her angry gaze locked on to his amused eyes, and Clint felt a jolt jump between them. Hot damn, he sat up a little straighter. There might be more to this filly than he'd imagined.

Laura, however, had not felt any similar connection as

she turned to appeal to their captain. "Sir, pretending to be Detective Marshall's wife seems unnecessary for this case, why we could—"

"It is completely necessary." Clark was only in his late forties, but the lines in his face and the ever-increasing amount of white in his salt-and-pepper hair proved to Clint that he was right in his own plan to return to his hometown before the constant unrelenting pressures of big-city policing had him looking the same. The captain shoved aside the salad he was having for lunch and poured two Advil capsules into his palm from his always open bottle.

Laura frowned. "You shouldn't take so many—"

She snapped her mouth shut when Clark glared at her.

He chewed the tablets and swallowed. "Trust me, if it was up to me, the last officers I would team up would be you two—not because I care what either of you thinks of the other, but because you are both new to my department and I don't particularly like either of you. Now, however, you're coming in useful. So you're going to do exactly what I say." He glared at them.

Clint kept on his good old boy face and Laura never twitched a muscle in hers. She was tough, he had to give her that.

Clark picked up a glass of murky greenish brown liquid and, holding his breath, swigged it. A newlywed, he'd taken to drinking the green bile as part of a health kick. He put down the glass and grimaced. "Damn, this stuff tastes so terrible it has to be good for you. Now, listen good while I go over the facts of the case—the faster I have you out of my office the better. Peter Monroe is target of the Special Financial Investigation's case," he nodded at the slim, blond-haired man.

"Peter Monroe of Monroe Investments?" Laura asked, a

note of admiration in her voice. "He started out with nothing and has a multibillion dollar empire today."

"That's him," the skinny man said. "Special Agent Vincent Garrow, SFI. I've been on the Monroe case for twenty months."

So he was right, Clint thought. Garrow was an accountant or some kind of financial expert. SFI were police officers with briefcases and business degrees working on insider trading, embezzlement, scams and other financial shenanigans. It was not a department Clint wanted to be part of. He preferred people to numbers. "He must be very good to have avoided being caught doing anything guilty in that time," Clint said. "In almost two years he must have at least cheated on his expenses."

Garrow ignored Clint and tossed a folder on Clark's desk. "This is everything on Monroe, including lists of his investments and businesses he's bought and sold."

Laura opened the file and scanned a few pages. As Clint suspected, she fit in with the pencil pushers. "Monroe's wealth is even greater than *Fortune* magazine said it was, but why do you think he's doing anything worth investigating?"

Garrow wiped his palms with his handkerchief. "We received a tip almost two years ago about Monroe laundering Russian mob money through his investment divisions."

"If the information was solid enough for SFI to begin a full-scale investigation," Clint asked, "why haven't you brought charges against him?"

Garrow leaned over Laura's shoulder and picked a piece of paper out of the file. Clint noticed Garrow linger, a little too long, close to Laura. Garrow saw Clint watching him and dropped his gaze. "Russian Mafia money definitely went through Monroe's companies, but we can't connect it directly to him. In fact, every piece of dirty money we've followed into Monroe Investments has been tied to a different division. We haven't been able to connect anything directly and specifically to Peter Monroe—only to five of his senior executives."

"So he's very smart—and you can't pin anything on him. I'm surprised you still have a full investigation on him," Clint said. "Why don't you arrest the suits and sweat them until one talks."

Garrow smiled sourly. "Our case isn't strong enough—the clues add up but broken down it's just circumstantial evidence. High-priced lawyers will poke enough holes in our case to keep each of our suspects out of jail. We want the brains behind the money." He stroked his upper lip and Clint wondered if he'd been on assignment recently where he'd worn a mustache. "We don't have a complete team on Monroe anymore. In fact, for the past six weeks, I've been the only investigator. I'm being reassigned in one week."

"So you came up with one last-ditch effort to find the incriminating evidence you need," Clint concluded.

"Last ditch is perhaps a little desperate sounding." Garrow straightened his tie.

"He's desperate," Clark interrupted. "The only solid piece of information the numbers guys have on Monroe is his psychological profile. Two years of investigation and they have absolutely nothing on him." Clark guffawed, a loud burst of noise, and then grinned in pleasure at another department's failure. Clint knew that like most cops, Clark resented the SFI's impressive budget and habit of stealing news headlines. "Two years and nothing. Nada. Zilch." He made a zero with his fingers. "That's why they've come crawling to us. Us ordinary cops with no special titles or secret budgets. The guys who are out there on the streets, taking it every day for the safety of the city of Chicago. Specifically for you two. The cowboy and the heiress."

Clint saw Laura move ever so slightly and almost leaned forward to stop her, but checked himself. Let her make her own bed. He'd always reckoned it was better to go along until he could figure out how to suit the circumstance to his own needs.

Laura smiled winningly at her boss. "Captain Clark, if I could interrupt here for a moment, I've studied financial—"

"No, you may not," Clark shouted.

The smile dropped from Laura's face, in fact Clint would have sworn she shut herself off. Clint didn't know any other way to describe how she was looking at their boss. She had just thrown off a switch in herself. She was still listening, but he could tell part of her wasn't there anymore.

"You may not say another word," Sam Clark continued. Clint could have told her there wasn't any point in trying to change their senior officer's mind, but she would never listen to his advice. As far as he could tell, Laura never listened to anyone's advice.

More importantly he wanted to hear more details of the case. This could very well be the opportunity he'd needed to get him back home. He'd spent the past year in Chicago and while he genuinely liked the windy city, he heard Texas calling to him more and more often.

If he and Laura were successful on this case, he might be promoted to Homicide, which was the best of the best. If he solved the case quickly, Captain Clark would have to recommend him for the spot. With his record in Dallas and his work in Chicago, he figured he was the prime candidate. Once he'd plugged in a year or two in Homicide, no one back home could ever claim that there was anyone more qualified than himself to be sheriff of Two Horse Junction. In fact the only downside to this whole situation was being forced to spend a lot of time with Laura Carter.

Mind, if she had to wear a couple of pretty dresses, hang off his arm and admire him, he didn't think the assignment would turn out all that bad. "Perhaps you could share with us exactly how the cowboy and the heiress fit into your investigation?"

Garrow nodded. "You're going to attend a society wedding and make contact with Peter Monroe."

"Who's getting married?" Laura asked.

"Penelope York and Kyle Chandler."

"Penelope York of York Construction?"

Garrow nodded. "Do you know the family personally?"

"No," Laura said. "I've never met them, but my uncle owns stock. He likes to talk about his investments. Have we been invited to the wedding?"

"Yes. I've made arrangements for your invitation. Since it's a big society event, your family connection," he looked at Laura, "was the entry we needed. The bride's father was more than happy to cooperate with the SFI, especially after we found a few irregularities with one of his deals. He's the only one who will know the two of you aren't married."

"So York gets his case closed and a cop from a good family on the guest list," Clint said. "Won't other guests know that Laura is a cop?"

"No," Laura said quickly. "People from my family's social set don't know I'm a cop."

"What do they think you do?"

"Nothing."

"They think you're just a party girl?" he asked disbelievingly. While he didn't much care for Laura, no one could deny she was a hard worker.

"Something like that." Laura pushed that errant strand of hair back into her braid. "What exactly are Clint and I supposed to do at the wedding?"

"With all the parties celebrating the nuptials it's a week-long affair. Donald York has gone full-out with the celebrations and the Chandler family has thrown in what money they have as well." Garrow waved the Monroe file at them accusingly. "Let me state the assignment more clearly. You're going to do more than make contact, you're going to become Mr. and Mrs. Monroe's new best friends." Garrow stared at the file he held in his hands. "We've had agents in his company studying every move Peter Monroe makes. Another operative became a social friend at his country club, but nothing. Hell, one of our best agents has spent hours shopping with Mrs. Monroe, but she doesn't know anything."

"Or she's too smart for your operative," Laura said, but the men ignored her.

"Clint and Laura Marshall are attending all the festivities of the York-Chandler wedding because the Yorks are important business associates. What's more, Donald York revealed that Monroe asked for Nicholas Vasili to be invited to the wedding ceremony and reception. Vasili is Russian Mafia. This is the closest we've ever been to getting Monroe and Vasili in the same room." Garrow's face grew animated as he revealed his case. "You two are going to figure out why Monroe wants Vasili at the wedding and uncover what they're up to. I suspect Vasili will be handing over another load of money for Monroe to launder through his companies—and you're going to catch them at it."

"That sounds about as likely as convincing a goat to

keep out of the garbage. Surely you have some kind of a better lead?" Clint asked, wondering what kind of a crazy assignment SFI was running.

Garrow mopped his brow with a white handkerchief. "This is our last chance. After this weekend the budget for this case is gone and I have to move on to a more likely candidate, but I want to get Peter Monroe."

"Why is he so important to you?" Laura asked.

Garrow looked at her, and for a second Clint thought he was going to tell the truth. But then Garrow said, "Because he's breaking the law."

Laura tilted her head to the left and studied the skinny man; clearly she, too, knew there was more to the story. "I don't understand why Clint and I need to pose as a couple to attend the wedding."

Sam Clark smiled with genuine pleasure as he studied the two of them. Clint didn't like the man's assessment. "Because you two, as a couple, fit Peter Monroe's fantasies. He's a boy from Jersey who grew up dreaming about the wild west. And cowboys."

"That explains him," Laura nodded toward Clint, "but how do I—"

"I'm from Texas," Clint interrupted. "That doesn't necessarily make me a cowboy."

"You could have fooled me," Laura muttered and stared at his boots.

Captain Clark took another swig of his green health drink, grimaced and pointed at Clint. "I don't care whether you can shoot a lasso or brand a haystack, you walk and talk like a cowboy and you're going to do your best to convince Peter Monroe you're the genuine article."

Clint wondered if he should point out his many years of police experience and several commendations, but decided not to give Clark more reason to punish him.

Laura crossed one elegant leg over the other and Clint noticed the other two men watching her. "Fine, Peter Monroe wants to play cowboy. I don't see—"

"If you'd let me finish a sentence you'd learn how you fit in. Damn, your last captain never said anything about you being such a chatterbox." Captain Clark ran a tongue over his teeth and grimaced as he tasted the remnants of the health drink. "Peter Monroe has two driving fantasies. He comes from a working-class family. His father was a factory worker and his mother was a waitress who used to make extra money by hiring herself out as service help for large society parties. Peter went with her, helping in the kitchen. Clearly that's when he became obsessed with high society. The longer a family's been in America the more impressed he is."

"But…" Laura started to interrupt again but quickly thought better of it.

"Yes?" The captain smiled at her predicament but Laura wisely decided not to ask how she fit into the scenario. At least the woman acknowledged the silver spoon she was born with.

Clint wondered what it would be like to be accepted because of one's family name. He was placing extraordinary demands on himself because of how badly his own family was perceived. His father had run off with the life savings of too many people in Two Horse Junction for him to be comfortable accepting the sheriff's job just because he was a good cop. He needed to show that he was a *great* cop.

Captain Clark smiled. "Unfortunately the Chicago P.D. isn't overrun by socialites. Luckily you transferred in. In fact it's good that the pair of you transferred in. I never dreamed I'd be happy to have a cowboy *and* an heiress working for me."

"I'm not…an heiress. My mother—" Another look at

Captain Clark's face and Laura stopped. She didn't bite her lip or fidget or anything. She just waited. Clint had to admit he liked how calm she was. It was the only thing he liked about Miss Nose-Stuck-Up-In-the-Air Laura Carter. When she'd transferred in from Boston he couldn't help but admire her beauty. But her ice-maiden attitude didn't appeal to him. He liked a woman who wasn't afraid to laugh out loud, who wasn't afraid to step in a puddle in order to cross the road. He preferred having a warm loving body in his bed, not a prickly cactus. She had about as much personality as a cactus, too.

It hadn't taken long for the rumors about her to spread. Clint didn't believe every story he heard, but there were so many of them about Laura Carter—and her relationship with her last boss—that he had wondered. She had been transferred out of Boston to Chicago very quickly—and under a cloud of secrecy. He knew how much paperwork was involved in switching from one city to another. It had taken him over a year to get himself approved for the move from Dallas to Chicago and that was only after he'd received a hero's thank-you for rescuing a kidnapped baby.

Clearly Little Miss Society had been sent to Chicago because of her misdeeds. He had seen her having dinner with the police superintendent just last week, probably thanking him for her job. Having dinner with the highest-ranked police officer in Chicago certainly didn't hurt her career. None of the other officers in their department had ever had such an honor, yet there she'd been, only a couple of months after joining the Chicago force.

He'd been having dinner with his own date, and unfortunately had become bored with her too quickly. He found that happening a lot recently. Probably because he missed home and was looking forward to finding himself a sweet Texas gal. A woman who appreciated a man like him.

The SFI agent took the center of the room. "The wedding of two of Chicago's most established families will be playing into Peter Monroe's psyche. It's the perfect opportunity for Mr. and Mrs. Marshall, the personification of his ultimate fantasy, to become his new best friends."

Laura frowned. "What you're saying makes a certain kind of logic, but once Clint and I worm our way into Monroe's circle then what? He's not about to confess his well-thought out criminal activities to us."

"The psychologists think he just might." Garrow shrugged. "I admit, the plan is kind of crazy, but it's our last chance. You can have all the paperwork on the profile, but our psychologist suggests that if Clint and Peter could become friends and then enter a one-upmanship contest— which Clint must win—Peter might show his own hand. At the very least he may be more careless than usual at the wedding when he meets with Vasili. This is the first time that we'll be able to prove that these two men have even been in the same room together. I need you two to be there and take advantage of whatever the situation may offer." Vincent ran a hand through his hair, "I realize this sounds desperate and—well it is. Basically you're going to have to improvise—including how to get Peter Monroe to show his hand."

Laura stood. "We'll do it."

When had she turned so sympathetic? Clint stood as well. "Well Captain, I'm honored to have the opportunity to work with an officer as fine as Ms. Carter. Plus, as my dear mother always says, the sooner we get started the sooner we'll be finished."

Laura glared at him.

"The most important thing is to convince Peter Monroe that you two are madly in love," the captain said.

"I've usually found the fillies do fall madly in love with me," Clint said in his very best Texas drawl.

Laura harrumphed. Clint slid an arm around her, hugging her to him. "Now, honey, was that any way to show enthusiasm for this project?"

She stiffened against him. He felt her take a deep breath and he counted to five before she disengaged herself and moved away from him slightly. It figured Laura didn't have to count to ten like a regular person; she regained her composure in five. "Cowboy, there's nothing I would like better than to be married to you for the weekend." She smiled sweetly and he felt incredible pain—and realized she'd ground one heel of her pump into his boot.

Determined to show her he wasn't the hick she thought he was, and wondering why he wanted to prove otherwise, he limped to the office door and opened it. She swept past him, her chin up in the air and her back ramrod straight as she marched away. He let his gaze fall to her buttocks which nicely filled out the tailored navy skirt but there was no seductive sway of her hips.

Damn, he had to admit she was beautiful, especially when she was mad at him, but she was not the kind of woman he was attracted to.

Laura Carter might be gorgeous but she was also a royal pain in the butt.

She kept going past his desk to the women's bathroom while he picked up his messages. His brother Ben had called, as had Amber, a working girl who sometimes had good tips. Naturally she hadn't left a number for him to return her call, but he knew that if it was important she'd find him.

Stan Lesky stopped at his desk and grinned. "Score man. You got assigned to Carter."

"Only for this assignment. There's nothing permanent about us as a team." In his year with the Chicago P.D. he'd had three different partners. Willy and he had partnered up for six months before Willy's retirement. Contrary to popular cop movies, they'd thrown a nice goodbye party and Willy had retired to the suburbs to annoy his wife. Then Clint had partnered with whoever was available, most often with Lucy Wong, a veteran of fifteen years in the department, and with Jeff Knight on his first rotation as a plainclothes officer. Despite the fact that Jeff Knight had grown up in Chicago, Clint knew he had never been as young or enthusiastic as Jeff.

It wasn't only the big city that had hard lessons to teach. Anyone looking at Jeff and Clint side by side at age twenty-two would assume Clint was the sophisticated, cynical man from the big city and optimistic Jeff the bumpkin from Two Horse Junction, Texas, population five hundred and eighty-seven.

Every year the population of Two Horse fluctuated by five to ten. Some years it decreased as the young people left; then it would swell again as some disillusioned souls came back home. Clint planned to increase the number by one very soon—his brothers needed him, and more importantly he needed to be back home. And once he was back he planned to find a nice local girl to marry—he knew his mother had a list of suitable single women—and to increase the population of his hometown even further with a houseful of kids. A sweet and loving wife he would treasure, look after and never leave. And he would be sheriff.

Sheriff in a small town was much better than being a detective in Chicago. Both jobs were important, he acknowledged, but back home he would know the people in his town. He'd be able to help in a real way—and be able to stop trouble before it grew out of hand. A small-town sheriff was a law enforcer, the first administrator of justice, a social worker, marriage counselor and role model.

Unlike his father he wanted the respect of his town. He loved his hometown but he needed its respect even more. When Sheriff O'Conner retired next year and Clint was offered the job, he wanted everyone in town to say that he was the best man for it. If he succeeded with this case—made some kind of breakthrough that the SFI had not—if he joined the homicide squad, then no one in Two Horse Junction could doubt that a full-fledged Chicago detective hadn't earned the position of sheriff.

Lesky grinned even wider, showing off his big shiny white teeth. The man could be found in the men's room flossing several times a day and recently he'd even bleached his teeth. "Carter is a fine piece of woman."

"More like an iceberg."

"Sometimes melting an iceberg can be appealing. All that fresh, untapped water." He wiggled his eyebrows.

"You're forgetting what happened to the *Titanic*. I, however, remember my history. My only interest in Laura Carter is whether or not she's a good cop."

"I'll bet she's good all right—at least that's what her old captain believed."

"That's a rumor," Clint replied, feeling a twinge of guilt at his own hypocrisy. "We're cops and are supposed to follow the facts, not gossip."

Lesky grabbed a chair and straddled it. "Fact number one, Laura Carter is a very beautiful woman. Fact number two, she moved up the chain of command faster than usual—faster than either you or me. Fact number three, she had a very close relationship with her captain in Boston."

Clint put his phone messages into his desk drawer. Lesky was tiresome. "That's pure speculation. The captain may simply have been her mentor."

"You'll be the one to judge how good she is...at police work." Lesky loved the sound of his own voice, and a small crowd was gathering around Clint's desk. The only way to stop Lesky was to let him finish.

Lesky looked around at his fellow officers. "Back to the facts. Fact number four, most of her unit believed she was having an affair with the captain, apparently including his wife. Fact number five, his wife began divorce proceedings and fact number six, because of Laura's family connections, she was transferred to us. How long did it take the paperwork to get you from Dallas to here?"

"A year."

"It took Laura two weeks."

Lesky had a valid argument but Clint never believed all the stories told about a person. Stories could be vicious and mean, even when they were based on truth.

He knew all about living with a reputation. "The facts could also indicate that she was—is—a damn fine cop."

"But that body. She's got great legs and—" he cupped a pair of imaginary breasts. "I'd love to lose myself in her body for a few hours."

"That's where we're different. I don't believe every rumor." Clint stood. "And trust me, the last thing I want to do is get my hands on Ms. Carter's body. Us Texas boys don't like frostbite." He pretended to shiver but saw that Lewsky wasn't smiling. He took a deep breath and turned around.

Clint reminded himself that his mama had taught him better. If you spoke your mind you had to accept the consequences. Laura stood in front of him, looking like she always did.

Her face wasn't flushed with anger, she didn't sweep her gaze disdainfully over him or even turn on her heel and stalk out.

Instead she looked cool and imperial. When she opened her mouth he braced himself for her cutting remarks. "What time do you want to pick me up tomorrow? It will make our cover story more believable if we arrive in one car."

He thought about apologizing, but she didn't look like she cared about what her colleagues thought of her. "Does noon work?" he asked instead.

"Can you make it a little later, say one-thirty? I have to organize a lot of clothes to play my part."

"Sure, that's okay." He opened his mouth and then closed it again.

She took a pen and piece of paper from his desk and wrote something on it. "My address. I'll be in the lobby at one-thirty." She handed the paper over to him and their fingers brushed. For a moment she eyed Lesky, then walked away.

This time Clint wanted to shiver for real. Laura Carter was even colder than he'd imagined.

No matter what the next few days held at the society wedding, it would be no honeymoon.

2

AT EXACTLY 1:25 p.m. of what she was sure was about to be the first of the worst four days of her life, Laura placed her two suitcases on the floor of the lobby of her building and looked out the front window. No cowboy on a white stallion.

She let out a pent-up breath, angry at herself. "You are a complete idiot and a juvenile one at that. You weren't even this bad when you had a crush on Kevin Beckins in seventh grade!" If she'd thought talking to herself would fix her unreasonable and unwanted crush on Clint Marshall, it didn't work. She'd never been so humiliated in her entire life. She had a crush on the cowboy. A crush!

Deliberately she replayed his words in her mind: *Trust me, the last thing I want to do is get my hands on Ms. Carter's body. Us Texas boys don't like frostbite.*

He hadn't even used her first name. He probably thought his tongue would freeze if he said her name out loud. He clearly considered her a stiff, prissy socialite.

She softly kicked one of her expensive suitcases with her even more expensive shoes. Sweetums whimpered in disagreement. "Baby, did I scare you? I'm sorry. Mummy was thinking about that nasty man we're being forced to spend a very long weekend with and I was trying to work out my frustration." She scooped the bundle of white fluff into her arms and adjusted the blue bow tied to the tiny dog's collar. "How's my little Sweetums?"

The dog squinted at her from under her long blond bangs and blinked. Laura kissed the top of the dog's head, amazed she'd come to care as much as she did for the ridiculous dog. She scratched Sweetums behind her ears and continued her running monologue. Sweetums liked to hear the sound of human voices. "If you were a real dog you'd bark. Or growl, or make some kind of loud noise— anything more than those little whiny noises you make when you sleep. Try barking for Mummy. Bark," Laura coaxed and then demonstrated by making a loud woofing sound. Sweetums looked at Laura curiously, opened her mouth and licked Laura's face.

"Well at least somebody likes me," she said ruefully and wished the cowboy's words hadn't hurt so much. Normally she liked her ice-princess routine. After all, she had spent years refining the image. She was very good at it. Because of it most men stayed far away.

Romantic involvements only confused most women's lives. At present count her mother had been married five times and each husband had had his own horrible qualities. Her mother continued to sail blithely across extremely dangerous seas from man to man, never noticing how much of her fortune each husband cost her or even more importantly how they destroyed her emotionally.

But Laura had noticed. And when she caught herself repeating her mother's pattern—completely changing herself to fit into her ex-fiancé's life—she'd stopped. Brian Simpson had almost been the biggest mistake of her life, but she'd gotten smart. Like mother, men were her weakness so she'd stopped dating. Joined the police force. Concentrated on her career. Exclusively.

She liked being a cop and she was good at it. She loved the challenge of figuring out a case: following obscure leads, interviewing witnesses until something clicked and she knew who had broken the law. She sympathized with Garrow's frustration; he knew that Monroe Investments laundered Russian Mafia money but he didn't have the evidence he needed to arrest Peter Monroe. When she'd first made detective, she and her partner had kept a case open for three years, working on it whenever they could squeeze in the time, until they'd finally made an arrest.

Once she'd proven she wasn't just playing at being a police officer, her colleagues had assumed that she would request a transfer to a unit like Special Financial Investigations. But while she appreciated the work Agent Garrow did, Laura preferred being on the street, helping ordinary people.

Being a good cop was her only priority. No man had been able to even chisel an inch of permafrost off her carefully developed exterior.

Until Clint Marshall.

A red sports car pulled up in front of her building and Clint unfolded his tall form from within. She watched and waited as he smiled at her neighbor, Mrs. Schwarz, and then held open the lobby door for her. He tilted his cowboy hat to the elderly woman and Mrs. Schwarz giggled as she passed him.

Laura's pulse quickened as she studied him from under her eyelashes. Clint was tall, well over six feet and since she was five-nine, he'd be the perfect height to kiss. He had broad shoulders and a well-muscled chest. She knew because he'd had his shirt ripped off once during a violent arrest and he'd spent ten glorious minutes in the squad room processing the paperwork before going to the locker room to change. She'd had to take a tight hold of her desk to stop herself from running her hands over his bronzed muscles.

Clint's long strides had him next to her and she took a

deep breath, inhaling the crisp masculine scent of Clint Marshall. She held Sweetums up to her face to mask her swirling emotions. Whenever she was around Clint, it always took a little longer for her to put on the face she showed the rest of the world.

"What in the blazes is that?" Clint demanded as he frowned at the bundle of white fluff in her arms.

"Her name is Sweetums." She raised the dog to his eye level.

Clint scowled at Sweetums. "What is it?"

"She's a dog."

"Darlin', I've got cats bigger than that and with a lot less fur."

Laura knew perfectly well the picture she and the Lhasa apso made. She was dressed in a pale blue suit, cradling a poofy white dog that in turn wore a bow that matched the exact shade of her blue suit. The image they presented was both sweet and ridiculous and, as she planned, Clint was looking at her in puzzlement. What was most important to Laura, however, was that she did not look like a member of Chicago's finest. Looking at Laura and her dog, people would assume she was a socialite with too much time on her hands rather than a hard-working police officer. Laura straightened the bow on her dog's head. "Sweetums is a Lhasa apso. She's not supposed to grow any bigger, which is a good thing, because she's just perfect as she is."

"Just big enough to fit into your pocketbook?"

She smiled sweetly and scratched Sweetums behind her ears. The dog panted and sighed. Ever since Sweetums's first owner had passed away, the dog loved to be petted and fussed over. Clint shook his head, his lips twitching and stroked Sweetums's head. The dog drooled. Of course, if Clint touched her like that, Laura reflected, she'd drool, too.

"The dog is named Sweetums?" Clint asked.

"Yes. Say hello to the nice man, Sweetums," she cooed into the dog's ear and waved one little doggy paw at Clint. Sweetums looked bored and yawned. "I guess she doesn't know what to make of a cowboy."

"I get that reaction a lot in Chicago. Although people are generally a little more polite."

"Is that why you turn the Texas drawl on and off?"

He shot her a quick look with his steel colored eyes but said nothing. He picked up her two suitcases. "Is this everything?"

"Yes." She patted Sweetums on the head and straightened the dog's bow again so that she wouldn't see Clint pick up her bags, see the rippling muscles in his arms or appreciate the view as he walked away from her. When she looked up she realized she was too late. Clint was already outside her building. She scrambled after him and caught up just as he put her two bags in the miniscule trunk of his convertible—his own bag was on the pretend excuse of a back seat—and then opened her car door.

"Darlin'," a mocking smile teased his lips as he gestured wide with his arm and helped her in. He touched her arm as she settled herself in, unaware that his touch marked her with greater power than any branding iron could have done.

As he walked around the car she looked at her left arm expecting to see the imprint of his fingers.

What was it about Clint Marshall that reduced her to a quivering mass of want? As Clint got in the car she pulled herself together—she'd spent enough evenings wasting her time thinking about Clint. She needed to establish a

professional working relationship with him, that was all.
But she was curious about him.

He started the sports car and pulled out into traffic.
Laura settled Sweetums on her lap and readjusted the
bow, choosing her words. If she was going to spend the
next four days with him, she didn't want to offend him,
but she wanted to understand him—for purely professional reasons, she told herself. She and Clint would be a
team for the next number of days. "With some people the
good old boy accent is so thick I can barely make sense of
what you're saying through all the y'alls and cow meta-
phors. But when you're with people you like, the whole
routine disappears."

She waited. Unlike how he behaved with most of their
fellow officers, Clint always turned on the Texas routine
when he spoke to her.

"Darlin', I just give the people what they want. They see
a Stetson and a pair of cowboy boots and have certain ex-
pectations—especially in a big established city like this."

She certainly understood his reasoning and she'd heard
the other women gossiping often enough about the handsome cowboy. One of the very young and gorgeous female cops on the force had stated that she couldn't imagine anything sexier than a cowboy in her bed.
Unfortunately that image had stuck in Laura's mind and
she'd spent too much time fantasying about his Stetson on
her pillow.

She realized that she and Clint shared a common trait:
she, too, gave people exactly what they expected.

Clint passed a car and then looked at her. "Why did you
bring that dog with you? Hotels have rules about not al-
lowing pets."

Sweetums settled herself more comfortably on Laura's
lap, drooled, sighed and closed her eyes. Luckily Laura

was familiar with this routine and had her handkerchief ready to wipe away the drool before it landed on her silk suit or the soft leather of the car seat. Most Lhasa apsos didn't drool, but after the trauma of losing her first owner the dog had stopped barking and started slobbering. She ran a hand along the calfskin. "Nice car," she said, avoiding his question.

"The department loaned it to me. Garrow must have some kind of pull—or else his bosses are giving him a last chance. They figured a red sports car would suit our image as wealthy newlyweds."

"It's lovely." Her mother's third husband, Larry, had loved cars and spent a lot of money filling a seven car garage. Laura had liked the vintage roadsters, and was quite sad when Larry and her mother had divorced and Larry had taken all the cars in the settlement. Laura missed the cars more than she'd missed Larry. As her mother was already in love with husband number four, she wasn't sure if her mother had noticed the absence of either.

Clint thumped the driving wheel of the red sports car. "Maybe you're used to a useless expensive car like this but back home this car wouldn't make it through the first pothole. You couldn't transport anything with it."

"Some things are designed to look good and go fast. Period. Not to haul around outhouses or maneuver around giant potholes. Maybe you should fix the roads back in Three Mule Station," she snapped and realized she'd lost her temper, deliberately making fun of Clint's hometown. She never, ever, lost her temper. But then again she never behaved like herself when she was around the cowboy.

"It's Two Horse Junction," Clint said without any heat. "I guess I prefer the practical to the purely decorative."

She knew he meant her, but she chose to ignore his comment. The knowledge that Clint Marshall didn't like her would not bother her. She ruffled Sweetums's bow, schooled her face not to reveal any emotion and pretended she didn't understand his real meaning. "Sweetums is a completely useful dog."

"Ha! She probably couldn't bark loud enough to call for help if someone was trying to break into your apartment."

"I have a doorman for that," she replied, but in truth she had been trying to teach Sweetums to bark for the past three months, ever since her neighbor, Mrs. Novak, had passed away. Laura had been the first person to enter Mrs. Novak's apartment, alerted by Sweetums's whining and scratching to find the elderly woman in her bed. The coroner had diagnosed heart failure. As Mrs. Novak hadn't had any relatives, or even many friends, Laura had handled the funeral arrangements. And, unable to turn the dog over to the city pound and an uncertain future, she had taken Sweetums home to live with her.

Laura had never had a dog, or a desire to saddle herself with a fluffy white useless creature that didn't even bark, but neither could she abandon the defenseless creature. So Laura took Sweetums home and tried to make her feel safe.

But after a month of silence, a month of the only sound of Sweetums making being an occasional pathetic whimper along with the excess drooling, Laura had taken the pooch to an animal psychologist. The therapist, after several expensive sessions, assured her that Sweetums just needed time to grieve for the loss of her mistress and to adjust to Laura. Sweetums would bark again, the doggie therapist had assured her and offered further counseling.

Laura declined and hired one of the kids in her building as a dog walker. Sometimes she worried that her long and erratic hours weren't fair to the dog, but Sweetums was delighted every time she came home.

Laura had to admit she rather liked having Sweetums to come home to. Never before in her life had anyone ever been excited to see her come home. In fact, Sweetums made her apartment feel much more like a home.

The dog was all the company she needed. Once she got over her inexplicable lust for the cowboy her life could return to normal. She pushed away the thought that she and Clint would be sharing a hotel room for the next four nights. What if he slept in the nude? No, she wasn't going to let her ice-princess façade chip one millimeter. Clint would never know how much time she had spent wondering what it would be like to kiss him…or anything else!

She continued playing with her dog's bow as she snuck covert looks at the cowboy. Mrs. Novak had liked to dress up the small dog and Sweetums seemed to enjoy it, so Laura occasionally tied a ribbon on her, or dressed her in one of the many sweaters Mrs. Novak had lovingly knit for her pet. Laura had brought along Sweetums's entire wardrobe for this assignment.

She shifted slightly in her car seat and stole another look at Clint Marshall. My, but he was a fine specimen of manhood, as Mrs. Novak would have said. And as Mrs. Schwarz had appreciated him when he had held open the door for her. Laura and all the little old ladies of Mortimer Manor would agree that Clint Marshall was the sexiest man they had ever seen.

Part of her wished that Clint found her attractive, that she could seduce him and have a passionate wild weekend. Wild, sweaty, hot sex. She would taste every inch of his broad chest that strained against his shirt, run her fingers through his dark hair, while his strong hands would caress her breasts and…she licked her dry lips.

Clint Marshall wasn't attracted to her.

She peeked another look at Clint. How she wished she

was the kind of woman who could sleep with him just once, or twice or even half a dozen times and let that be it!

Instead she knew her weaknesses. If she gave in, Clint Marshall would be the biggest mistake she could ever make. But only if she let down her defenses and let him know even for one second how much she wanted him. The state of Texas would host a Cowboys Getting in Touch with their Feelings convention before she would ever admit to her lustful fascination with Clint Marshall.

She wasn't the kind of woman who could have a fling without regrets, but she stupidly fell in love with whatever man she was with and let herself become distracted from her goals. It had happened with Brian. It could happen again. She was weak when it came to men.

She liked being a cop. She was good at being a cop. And despite the rumors that had followed her from Boston, the other officers were beginning to think she might be okay as well. She knew she had a lot of ground to cover before her colleagues believed her quick promotions had been because of her skills at detection rather than in the bedroom, but she was on the right track. The absolute worst thing she could do for her career would be to have a fling with Clint while on the society wedding assignment. She should be relieved that Clint found her repulsive.

It was much safer to talk about the dog. "Sweetums has been through a lot recently and was traumatized by the death of her first owner. The animal therapist said she'd start barking when she finished grieving."

"A doggie shrink." Clint shook his head as he shifted gears, and Laura wished his hand was on her leg. "We sure do live in different worlds, Princess." He reached over and patted Sweetums's head, while Laura tried not to notice how close his hand was to her thigh.

"How did you finally figure out that burglary case?"

Clint asked suddenly. "It had been passed around the department for a year before you took it over."

"I got lucky because Captain Clark assigned me all the grunt cases. The small-business burglaries and the purse snatchings."

"Every other detective was thrilled *not* to have those cases."

"I was the new guy, I had to pay my dues." Laura shrugged. "Anyway, I was checking out the various pawn shops to see if any of the items from the purse snatchings might have ended up there. I know muggers usually take the money and ditch the bag, but sometimes women have jewelry in their purse. Instead I found personal items stolen from the businesses that had been robbed over a year ago. That made me realize the thief was very local and someone who was willing to wait a long time to fence the personal items he took. Mostly he stole laptop computers and fax machines, but every once in a while the thief wasn't able to resist jewelry, expensive photo frames or other personal items."

"So the thief is local and patient. Then what?"

Laura could feel him watching her, but she continued to pet Sweetums and stare straight out the window. "The most reasonable assumption was that the thief didn't steal full-time for a living, because of how long he would wait to pawn the items. So I tried to think of someone who would go into a lot of offices on a regular basis so he'd know what was where. And then when I was in a pawn shop the watercooler guy made his delivery."

"That's what made you realize it was the water delivery guy?"

"Him or someone like him." Laura had been delighted that she'd been able to solve a burglary case that had sat open for a year. Clark had even grudgingly told her she'd done a good job. "I realized it was the water delivery guy when he asked what case I was working on and whether I'd heard anything about the local burglaries. He wanted to talk about himself. I didn't have enough for a warrant so I staked him out for a week and saw him break into a real estate office. I had him."

"A week's stakeout? There's no way Captain Clark would have approved that."

"I used my own time."

Clint pulled the car in front of the hotel, the Chicago Regal, one of the city's oldest and most elegant buildings. The York-Chandler wedding had reserved most of the rooms in the hotel. Laura looked at the gracious building, surprised the drive had passed so quickly.

He turned to her. "You're very determined. We're going to need that on this case."

She didn't wait for Clint to open her car door, but scrambled out. Sweetums looked around excitedly and made a high-pitched squeaking sound. Laura held her breath as she listened for any sound that could be called a bark, but Sweetums squeaked again and stopped.

She turned back to watch Clint wrestle his bags out of the back seat. A bellboy loaded them onto a waiting cart and the valet slid into the front seat of Clint's car.

"Woowee, Sugar, this here looks like a mighty fine hotel."

Clint draped a casual arm around her shoulder and a surge of warm pleasure washed over her.

Her reaction to Clint Marshall confused and surprised her. She'd dated since she was fifteen but she'd never experienced such a strong sexual attraction to any man as she did to Clint. She wanted him.

Ever since she'd first laid eyes on him six months ago, her dreams had been filled with erotic fantasies starring

Clint. Too often she caught herself staring at his muscular forearms, the fine hair on his hands. She even admired his easy camaraderie with his colleagues. His drawl reduced her to a pool of longing. A mass of quivering Jell-O.

She stiffened under his arm. For the sake of her pride, she wasn't about to let Clint suspect even an inkling of her feelings toward him.

Clint leaned in and whispered in her ear. "Relax, Princess. We're the happy couple—everything Peter Monroe's subconscious wants to be. We have to look deliriously happy together."

"We're not big on overt public displays of affection in my family or my social set," she said smoothly, annoyed at herself for telling him anything about herself. It wasn't in her nature to confide in others, especially near-strangers.

Maybe that was Clint's appeal for her, she considered as Sweetums stretched forward and sniffed Clint's leather jacket. He was so different from all the men she'd known, especially those from her upper-class background.

A cowboy would shock her mother clear down to her pedicured toes.

Wasn't she a little old at twenty-seven to be going through a rebellious stage? Laura wondered.

Clint's warm breath continued next to her ear. "Besides I'm looking forward to you talking that little dog's way into the hotel."

"Watch me." She smiled sweetly and walked briskly into the hotel, cooing to Sweetums every step of the way, all too aware of Clint directly behind her. She wished she was the kind of woman who could swing her backside, instead she smiled at the doorman who scrambled to open the door for her, all the time pretending she was her second cousin, Mindy, who traveled with an entourage of pets, including a potbellied Vietnamese pig, to the most exclusive hotels.

She sailed through the lobby, Sweetums's bow flapping in the breeze, and went straight to the executive check-in. Luckily there was no one else waiting and she bestowed her most gracious look on the young clerk behind the desk. She smiled. "What a charming hotel you have, you must be very proud."

The young man looked confused but he recovered. "Thank you."

"And you're so young to be in charge." She looked at his name tag. "Ralph. May I call you Ralph? I'm Laura Marshall and this gorgeous man behind me is my husband Clint." She turned to Clint. "Say hello to the nice young man, darlin'," She drawled the last word in a fine imitation of his Texas twang.

Clint pushed back his cowboy hat and grinned. "Howdy."

"This is Sweetums." Laura placed the dog on the counter, fussed with the blue bow, continuing blithely as Ralph blanched. Sweetums panted and drooled on top of the marble countertop. "Oh, she really likes you, Ralph, but then again Sweetums has always had exquisite taste."

Ralph blushed. "I'm sorry ma'am but—"

"Oh no, please don't call me *ma'am*. It makes me feel..." she shivered and said in a low voice, "...matronly." She leaned in closer, engulfing him in a wave of perfume. "You don't think I look matronly do you?"

The top of Ralph's ears turned pink. "No. You're beautiful." He gulped for breath. "Er, I mean—"

"No need to apologize for a compliment, young man." She leaned in a little closer and caught Ralph's eyes with her own, letting him fantasize for a moment about her. "But you'll be wanting to do your job. You can look us up in that computer now. We have a suite. Mr. and Mrs. Clint Marshall."

Ralph began typing into his computer, his gaze flickering between the screen and the dog. "Got it." He looked at her apologetically. "I'm afraid the hotel has a policy against animals."

"A very good policy it is, too." She straightened Sweetums's ribbon. "Imagine animals in a hotel. Whatever do some people think of?"

Ralph's ears turned red. "I meant pets. I'm afraid we don't allow pets of any kind."

Laura smiled at him. "Of course not. It's a very sensible policy. I knew I liked this place. Didn't I say so as soon as we saw the hotel. I said, 'Clint, honey, this looks like a first-class establishment.' Didn't I say that, dear?"

"You sure did, honey pie," Clint agreed from behind her.

She heard the laughter in his voice, but she refused to turn around and glare at him. Instead, she continued to smile sweetly at Ralph.

Ralph's ears reddened even more as he swallowed and looked again at Sweetums. "I'm afraid we can't, I mean—" he faltered as he pointed to Sweetums. The dog yawned and drooled on the marble countertop. "Your pet..."

She picked up Sweetums and kissed the top of the Lhasa apso's head. "Sweetums isn't a *pet*, she's part of the family."

"She's a dog," Ralph persisted.

Laura covered the dog's ears. "Ssh, you mustn't say those words around her. Sweetums has *species* issues."

Clint made a curious sound, but she ignored him. She'd told him she was going to get Sweetums into the hotel and she was enjoying playing the part of cousin Mindy. Perhaps this odd sense of power was why Mindy traveled with her animal menagerie. "Ralph, I thought this was a first-class hotel. I hope you're not about to change my impression within the first five minutes. We're here for the York-Chandler wedding. Sweetums goes everywhere I go. Surely you don't want me to tell the happy families that you're refusing to let us stay?"

"Of course not, Mrs. Marshall, but your do—"

"Not that word," she held up her hand. "Species issues." She rubbed Sweetums behind her ears and Ralph gulped.

"Sweetums is against hotel policy," Ralph said as he tugged on an ear.

"Of course I understand that for your *average d-o-g,*" she spelled out the letters, "this is a very good policy. But Sweetums isn't average." She leaned a little closer and stroked Ralph's cheek, her hand lingering just beneath his earlobe. "Sweetums will be very good. No one will know she's even here. I promise," she breathed and raised her blue eyes to his and held him. She watched worry about his job and desire to please her cross his face and his ears wiggled. She held herself very still, every inch of her regal family's genes giving her strength.

Just as she was afraid she might have lost him, Ralph hit some keys on the keyboard and nodded to the bellboy behind them. "They're in the honeymoon suite."

"We are?" Laura couldn't keep the shocked surprise out of her voice. She cast a suspicious look at Clint, but he smiled blandly. There was absolutely no way she was going to spend four nights together with Clint in the honeymoon suite. "Won't the bride and groom want that suite?"

"They have separate rooms until the wedding and are leaving for the Bahamas right after the reception."

"How sweet and old-fashioned," she muttered.

"Honeybunch, I reserved us the honeymoon suite." Clint had stepped forward and he hugged her to his side. Her face was pressed into his leather jacket and she couldn't breathe. She tipped her face up and saw Clint smiling down on her like he'd won a prize. "I thought it would be nice to combine a little honeymooning of our own with this wedding shindig."

"How lovely. You should have told me." She tried to move away from him but his hold was like a vise.

"Don't worry, I packed my favorite negligee."

She bared her teeth at him. She kicked him in the shins, but his cowboy boots protected him while her expensive shoes offered her no protection. "Ouch, er, a second honeymoon. What a nice idea."

"Well, Sugar, nothing's too good for you. And since we never saw anything of Paris on our first honeymoon, I thought we could do things proper this time."

"Chicago isn't Paris."

"No but this time we'll leave the hotel room occasionally." He winked.

"Darling, you're making my toes curl in anticipation." She managed to loosen an arm and elbowed him in the side. Clint let go of her and grinned, enjoying her discomfort. Laura scooped her dog back into her arms to keep Clint away from her.

"I married a big strong man, didn't I, Sweetums?" She stepped a little closer to Clint and rose on tiptoe so that her lips were next to his ear. Irritated with the man beyond belief, but also unable to resist, she brushed her teeth across his lobe and had the satisfaction of feeling his body stiffen. His hands shot out and grabbed her arms. Before he could pull her away from him, she whispered "Peter and Cassandra Monroe at four o'clock."

His tight grip turned into a caress as he turned slightly

so that he was able to see the couple. "Did he notice us?" he asked against her ear.

She ignored the shiver his warm breath sent down her spine. "He looked over in our direction, but that's it."

"The whole point of our being here is for him to notice us. Let's make sure he does."

Before Laura had any idea what he planned he took Sweetums out of her arms and she found herself holding her breath thinking: *he's going to kiss me.* She'd considered that at some point over the festivities she and Clint might kiss, but she'd been sure she would know when it was going to happen and have time to prepare herself. She didn't want to give Clint any inclination of her true feelings for him.

She took a deep breath, which steadied her nerves. She smiled at him, ready for his mouth to descend over hers and her world to turn upside down.

Her world turned upside down. She felt her feet leave the ground and found herself staring at Clint's very attractive behind. Sweetums was decorously cradled against Clint's chest while she was tossed over his shoulder like a sack of potatoes. Laura didn't care who heard her. "Put me down you big oaf!"

Clint slapped her backside and strode across the lobby in huge man-eating steps. Laura ground her teeth in frustration as she realized every last person in the hotel lobby—including Peter Monroe and his wife Cassandra— were staring at them. Clint pushed the elevator button. She could hear the grin in his voice as he announced to the hotel lobby, "I've got me a first-class filly and we're going to have a second honeymoon. Not that the first one ever really ended."

As Laura raised her head she saw Cassandra say something to Peter Monroe and the target of their assignment smiled as he looked at her. Then he winked at her.

The elevator doors opened and Clint strode inside, turned around and stopped the bellboy who was about to follow them with their luggage. "Take the next car. The missus and I want to be alone for a minute."

The bellboy obeyed, his mouth hanging open, and the doors closed behind them leaving her and Clint alone in the elevator.

"Put me down."

"If I put you down, are you going to kill me?"

"Yes."

He shifted her weight slightly on his shoulder. "Then I can't put you down until you promise not to hurt me."

"You hoisted me over your shoulder like a bag of wet laundry."

"More like flour really. You're not nearly heavy enough or lumpy enough for wet laundry."

"Put me down!" she demanded.

"Not until I have your word."

"You can't keep me on your shoulder forever."

Clint pushed the Stop button.

"Don't do that. They're going to think we're..."

"We're what?" he drawled the question in his most obnoxious Texan twang as one hand traced a circle on her inner knee.

Laura clenched her teeth together to stop herself from moaning. She tried to kick her leg but his arm was like a band of steel across her upper thighs. "You know very well what they'll think."

To her surprise she found herself back on her feet. She straightened out her skirt as the blood drained from her head.

"Well, at least we got Peter Monroe's attention," Clint said.

She knocked him back with both hands hard against his chest. Or rather she meant to knock him back but he didn't move. Instead he caught her hands in his and held her captive. How did this man do this to her? She was far too aware of her racing pulse. Hopefully he would account it to anger and not lust.

"I apologize," he said, surprising her again. He let go of her hands and leaned against the wall. "If Peter Monroe really has a subconscious desire to be a cowboy, then he got a taste of what people believe Texans are."

She sighed. "Overgrown Neanderthals who think they're charming?"

"Yes."

She understood all about being mistaken for your image and her anger deflated. "You do get ribbed about being a cowboy cop. Okay, maybe you did have a good idea—but no more good ideas like that without consulting me first. I don't appreciate having my butt stuck up in the air for everyone to ogle."

"It's such a cute butt how could they help but admire it?"

"Don't try to sweet-talk me, cowboy. I'm not falling for any of your good old boy routine." She pushed the Start button. "And don't even think about manhandling me again."

"What about when we get to the honeymoon suite? It's customary for the groom to carry the bride over the threshold."

Clint stood watching her, humor lighting his chiseled face, making him so handsome she had to catch her breath. She turned away from him and pressed their floor button again, wishing she could transport herself safely

behind doors and away from Clint. She put on her best
frosty expression as she raked him from head to toe. "It's
also customary for the groom to live through the night.
You try any funny business and you won't."

3

THE NEXT MORNING after an uncomfortable sleep on the couch of the suite's living room—his mother had raised a gentleman after all—Clint followed Peter Monroe to the gym and then to the hotel barber and wondered if he should have let Laura carry through on her threat to put him out of his misery. He'd give up his best horse to be on any other assignment right now.

Last night they'd dined in the restaurant, two tables away from the Monroes, but despite the fact that Clint had worn his cowboy hat and Laura, with her hair twisted in a top knot, had worn a pastel green dress without a flounce or trim of any kind—so plain and simple he knew it had to cost a fortune—the Monroes hadn't noticed them.

The real problem, however, was that *he* had noticed Laura all throughout dinner.

While Laura toyed with the stem of her wineglass, she had asked, "Do you think they really wanted a society heiress on this case or do you think Clark was just looking for another opportunity to give me a dumb assignment in the hopes I'll quit?"

"Darlin', working with me is never a punishment," he teased, and smiled at her, imagining himself nibbling on her long slender neck. He took her hand and stroked his thumb over her knuckles, just in case Peter Monroe was watching them. Leaning in slightly so that he could smell her perfume he whispered, "It's pure pleasure. Guaranteed."

With her cheeks flaming she had snatched her hand out of his, and Clint had been surprised she could be so easily flustered. Surely she was used to flirting with the young men of her social circle. Or maybe she'd learned to exert caution when it came to cops.

He'd been surprised yesterday when he'd held her in his arms to discover a number of nice curves, but there were a lot nicer and easier women he preferred to spend time with. Since he was only going to be in Chicago long enough to get the promotion, there was no point in getting involved with anyone before he went back home. Not that an uncomplicated affair wouldn't be nice, especially if the sex was good, but there was no such thing as an uncomplicated relationship with a woman. And Laura Carter was even more complicated than most women.

Captain Clark had given Laura the cases that demanded the longest hours and had the least chance of being solved but she hadn't complained. Instead she had done her job. He had to admit he admired her spirit. And now that he was thinking about Laura he realized she had closed the docket on an impressive number of her cases. Her average rivaled his.

Like everyone else he'd been so caught up in her image as an ice princess that he hadn't really paid much attention to her work. Coming from a family that had been judged by their father's larcenous history, he had fought to be accepted for his actions, not his father. Except he'd judged Laura on her reputation and image, not her actions.

Last night, after he'd lost the coin toss to see who was sleeping in the big honeymoon bed and who got the couch, when he'd finally finished reading the Monroe file, he'd found himself thinking about Laura rather than the case. She hadn't revealed much about herself except to say her mother was divorced and she'd grown up in Boston. Instead they'd spent the hours discussing various schemes on how to befriend Peter Monroe and get him to confess all. As they'd debated the merits of Clint rescuing Peter from the charge of a runaway horse versus Laura claiming the Monroes as part of her family tree, they'd laughed at the ridiculousness of their assignment.

Clint had spent far too much time for the rest of the miserable night on the too-small couch wondering exactly what Laura's scent was and when and where she and her boss had made love. He had wondered if she had a lover now. He wondered why he was wondering.

In the morning he'd woken up to find something warm and soft on his chest, someone nibbling on his chin. "Laura," he'd muttered and opened his eyes to see Sweetums smiling at him. The dog drooled on his face and Clint placed her on the floor just as Laura had walked into the living room.

"Oh." Her eyes had darted to his bare chest and then she'd scooped the dog into her arms. "Did Sweetums wake you up?" Laura had had shadows under her eyes as if she too had been kept awake by uncomfortable thoughts.

He'd wondered if she spent any time thinking about him as anything other than a hick cowboy. As neither of them had thought of any brilliant plan or found anything in the files that Garrow had missed they agreed that Laura would head to the hotel's spa in an attempt to bond with Cassandra Monroe. Laura had bribed one of the workers into telling her when Cassandra had her appointment. After grabbing an apple and juice off the room service cart she had remembered to order last night, Laura had left their suite looking classy and beautiful, dressed in a pair of fleece pants and white T-shirt and carrying a large tote bag.

Clint had wasted his morning tailing Peter as he spent an hour and a half in the gym, followed by a haircut, all the while taking at least half a dozen phone calls. Since Garrow had had Monroe's cell phone tapped and had never learned anything incriminating, Clint hadn't learned anything except that Peter liked to talk business, all day, every day. As far as Clint could tell, the only time Peter Monroe wasn't thinking about his company was when he was with his wife.

Back in the lobby of the hotel, Clint hid himself behind a newspaper as more wedding guests—he could tell by their gifts—arrived and saw Peter checking his watch. He was meeting someone for a late lunch, Clint guessed. Peter's face lit up as he waved at his wife as she came toward him. She kissed him lightly on the lips and straightened the collar of his polo shirt under his casual jacket. They were joined by the Yorks, the parents of the bride, and the proud hosts of the wedding. Tonight, the groom's parents, who were also Peter Monroe's cousins, were hosting a dinner in the rooftop ballroom, to be followed by a full-day cruise on Lake Michigan for all the young people who had arrived for the wedding. Clint was sure he and Laura would be able to avoid the cruise.

The York-Chandler nuptials were being celebrated in high-society style. The four days leading up to the wedding were filled with dinners and luncheons, a bachelor party and a bridal tea. If needed, Donald York, the young bride's father, was prepared to introduce the Marshalls to the Monroes, but Clint and Laura had agreed it would be better if they could find some more interesting, unconventional way to capture the self-made millionaire's attention. Yesterday's antics in the lobby hadn't been enough. It seemed that with five hundred wedding guests Clint and Laura could blend in too easily. They would need to think of something dramatic to stand out.

For a wedding at Two Horse Junction all you had to do was show up at the church on time, and then make sure you had enough food and whiskey to feed everyone in town back at your house. His mother had written that Ellen Lansing and Tom Conner's wedding celebrations had lasted well through the next day. Clint knew that was because a number of the young men in town had consoled themselves at losing their chance with the most beautiful girl in town by partying long and hard, including his brother, Ben.

He watched the two couples head into the Monarch Restaurant on the hotel's main floor and followed at a discreet distance. The waiter seated them at a table by the window. There was no way Clint could sit anywhere close to them without sticking out like a fox in a henhouse, so he went back out into the lobby.

Clearly the shrinks had it wrong when it came to Peter Monroe and his fantasies. Money could be the most powerful allure of all.

The couches in the lobby were spindly looking sticks of furniture that felt as uncomfortable as they looked. He decided to check out the bar and have a beer instead. The lounge was filled with the same muted light of hotel lounges around the world. A waitress dressed in a white blouse and short black skirt carried drinks from the bar to the round tables. A cluster of businesswomen attending a convention sat at one table while two solitary men sat alone at tables next to each other. Clint walked up to the bar and asked for a beer.

Maybe he should somehow ingratiate himself with the

groom's family. No. He wasn't very good at ingratiating himself in with anybody and so far he hadn't seen Peter Monroe spend any time with the groom or his distant relations. Clearly the wedding was a social obligation, but not a loving reunion.

Nicholas Vasili wasn't scheduled to arrive until the day of the wedding. Clint cursed under his breath. How were he and Laura supposed to make any kind of a case against Peter Monroe?

The head shrinks definitely had to be wrong about the man. Clint decided to proceed according to Garrow's plan for the rest of the day, but if he and Laura didn't make any connection tonight at the York dinner they might as well call Captain Clark and tell him to pull them off the case.

No, he'd never asked to be let off a case and he wasn't about to start. He had to think of something to make them connect with the Monroes. The psychological profile must have some validity, but he and Laura needed to make an impression. Something different, but what? He wondered if Peter liked silly dogs with floppy bows.

If he had an iota of his father's famous charm he and Peter would be friends and he'd be pocketing a check for an investment.

"Marshall, is that you?"

He looked up. Reflected in the glass behind the bar was Amber, whose message he had stuffed into his desk drawer. He'd arrested Amber once and let her off a second time after she'd helped him find a perp who enjoyed hurting the youngest of the working girls. Now that he saw her, he realized he hadn't spoken to her for several months. Nor was the Regal the kind of hotel that tolerated working girls of Amber's caliber.

Amber's shiny raincoat hung open, revealing a burgundy dress that clung to her thin body. Her black vinyl boots added three inches to her short stature. She shifted the package she was carrying in one arm. "Your pig friend said I could find you here. I thought if I hung around the lobby long enough I could find you and sure enough I saw you walking into the bar. What are you, undercover or something?"

"Who told you I was here?" he asked, his eyes searching for somewhere private to talk.

"The cop with the shiny teeth who's always sweating and looking at me like he's going to jump me any second. Lesky." She wrinkled her nose as if she smelled something bad. "That guy makes my old pimp look decent. Don't worry about me being here—I won't get in the way, but I had to talk to you. It's urgent." She bit her bottom lip as she reached out and touched Clint's arm. "I really need your help."

Clint looked back at Amber. She was petrified of something, but her presence jeopardized his cover. Plus, as soon as he was back in the precinct he was going to kill Lesky. "How did you convince Lesky to tell you where I am?"

"I told him I had to talk to you—that Johnny might hurt me really badly...or worse, if I couldn't see you."

"Lesky could have contacted me himself." Clint's gaze narrowed as he studied the girl. "What else did you tell him?"

Amber grinned at him and Clint realized that beneath the makeup she was rather pretty. "Okay, you're smart. I told Lesky that we'd been having a...a relationship and that I needed to see you immediately."

"You told Lesky we were sleeping together?" Clint gritted out between clenched teeth.

"I let him think it. And because Lesky wants to sleep with any girl who's pretty enough he totally believed me. It's easy to trick a man with his own weaknesses." Amber shrugged. "Luckily Lesky isn't all that smart. Another thing he and Johnny have in common." She took a deep breath and stared at the bar's countertop. "I told him about my baby...."

"Lesky thinks you're pregnant? And that I'm the father?" Clint shook his head in frustration. "I hope you have a damn good reason for finding me. Has Johnny been bothering you again?" He was annoyed with her, but worried about why Amber needed him so urgently. Johnny, her pimp, was mean and stupid and enjoyed hitting the women who worked for him.

"This isn't your usual beat. What are you doing here?" She shifted her package from one arm to the other.

"I'm attending a wedding." He took a closer look at her face. She sported a purple bruise on her left cheek "Looks like business hasn't been all that good to you recently."

She touched her bruised cheek. "It's Johnny. He thinks I'm holding out some of my earnings on him."

"Are you?"

"No, I give that good-for-nothing everything and then he rips me off."

"You should find yourself a different line of work." Clint said the line automatically and took another swig of the beer. Amber had been on the street for three or four years. In his experience the only girls a cop could rescue were the ones starting out.

"I am going to do something different with my life." Amber raised her chin and met his gaze levelly. To his shock he saw determination there—and no glassy after-effects of drugs or booze.

"You're serious?"

"Dead serious. Look at this dress I'm wearing, it goes to my knees."

He had to admit it was more conservative than the

barely-there dresses she usually wore. Amber put her package on the bar. "Yo, bartender, am I invisible or something?"

The bartender moved toward them. His gaze swept over Clint dismissing him and settling on Amber. "We have a policy against serving working girls. The Regal is a first-class establishment, we don't want your kind here. Leave before I call the cops."

Amber's cheeks turned as red as her name. "Listen here, jerk-off—" she grabbed the bartender's tie and pulled his face down to the wood of the bar.

Clint pried open her death grip on the tie and let the bartender loose. No one in the bar was paying any attention to them. He flashed his badge. "She's with me. Get the lady a drink."

The bartender scowled. "What do you want?"

Amber glanced at Clint's beer longingly. "I'll have a Coke."

"Nothing in it?" the bartender asked suspiciously.

"Did I ask for anything in it?" She growled and made a move for him but Clint caught her by the shoulders.

"Easy does it, Amber. The guy doesn't have any manners, but I remember a time when you would have had a double vodka in that Coke."

"More like triple." She smiled at him and it hit him that she couldn't be any older than twenty-one. The bartender put a glass on the bar and she took a sip of her drink and touched the item she had wrapped in a blanket. "But that was before."

"Before what?"

She shifted the wrappings on what he had thought was some kind of tote bag and in shock he realized that it wasn't a bag but a baby carryall. "Before this little sweetheart came into my life."

The pink face of a baby scrutinized him then smiled. Its blue eyes were the exact shade and shape as Amber's.

"It's a baby!"

"I guess that's why you're such a good cop," Amber said, as she looked at him as if she were judging something about him. "Nothing gets past you." She brushed the baby's cheek, and then looked at Clint. He could see shadows under her eyes from lack of sleep. "I...well I was hoping that you could help me with Johnny."

Clint continued staring at her with amazement. The life she'd been living was hard enough, but having a child only complicated it even further. From the look of maternal love on Amber's face he could tell she planned on keeping the baby. His gut tightened as he remembered growing up dealing with his father's bad reputation. What would it be like for Amber's child? Should he try to convince her to give up the baby to people who could look after it better?

Another look at Amber's face told Clint there was no way she would give up her child. And he knew he had to help her.

"The only way I can really help you is if you quit the business. You have a child to worry about now."

"I want to, it's just not that easy. I don't what my baby growing up with the same kind of crap that I grew up with. He's going to have a better life." She looked at her child with fierce determination, then turned back to Clint. "I've got some money set aside. I'm going to learn computers and then get a regular job."

"I thought Johnny got all your money."

"Yeah, well, maybe I managed to keep a little." She finished her drink. "I was thinking maybe you could help me find out about the school stuff."

"I know people who can help," he said and waited for

her to reveal what she really needed from him. "I'll give you my number, call me in five days and I can set you up with a case worker." Clint pulled out his card and scrawled his cell phone number on the back.

She took the card and put it into her purse. "I don't want any social worker trying to take away my baby."

"The woman I'm thinking of is willing to break a few rules. Why don't you tell me what else you want."

"Johnny's threatened to hurt my son if I don't do what he wants. He said he would take away my baby—give him to some people he knows." The baby squawked and Amber picked him up, rocking him back and forth in her arms. "But I know what he really wants is to sell my child for cash—and keep me working for him." The baby scrunched up his nose and made another high-pitched sound. "That's why I took a chance at finding you here. Johnny and I had a huge fight and I got scared. I know he's after me and he's going to take my baby." Amber blinked her eyes several times. "That's why I had to see you right away. Please, can you help me?"

As the baby continued making an alarming sound, Clint tried to decide how he could help Amber. "There are some people I can call who can get you out of Chicago to someplace safe." The baby continued making a series of squeaks. "Is something wrong with it?"

Amber patted her son on the back. "You don't know much about babies do you? Don't you have any younger brother or sisters?"

"I have younger brothers but I never changed their diapers. Mama didn't believe in letting anyone look after her babies except herself."

"Yeah? Well your mama should have trained you better. My son is hungry. Here," she thrust the baby toward him, "hold him."

Clint found his hands full of baby. The baby didn't look any happier with the situation than he was. He looked up to see Amber fiddling with the front of her dress. "You're not going to breastfeed him are you? Here?" His words sounded unnaturally high to his own ears.

Amber sighed. "You really are in the dark ages, Texan."

"We should at least take a table in the corner."

"I'm surprised you can be shocked so easily, but okay," Amber stood up, "let's go somewhere a little more private. Then if you can tell me who to call, I will. I'm so grateful that you're willing to help me. I really didn't know who else to turn to."

Clint stood with her and spied a table behind the piano, it would offer a lot of privacy. "Over there," he suggested and started toward the dark table.

"Damn, my purse," Amber said and turned back to the bar. Clint headed toward the table where no one would be able to see him.

"Let go of me!"

He turned to see Amber yelling at a stringy-haired man who'd grabbed her by the arm. "You're coming with me," the scrawny man snarled. "Did you really think I wouldn't find you?"

"No!" Amber pulled her arms loose. "I'm not doing anything with you, Johnny." She shot a quick look at Clint and then took a deep breath. "I'm not working for you anymore, so you might as well leave."

Johnny slapped Amber across the face. The blow knocked her back and she raised her hand to her cheek—the cheek that was already bruised. "Bastard," she spat out.

As Clint started forward, the bartender surprised him by jumping from behind the bar and twisting the man's arm behind his back. "What the hell?" Johnny began.

"No one slaps a woman in my bar." The bartender began to push the thug out of the bar. Amber looked at the pair of them and then at Clint. With the baby in his arms he'd started forward and then remembering the baby stopped. Now he was impressed with the foolish bartender and wondered where the heck the hotel security was.

"You think by hiding that kid I won't find him," Johnny shouted. "I'll find the both of you and you won't see that brat of yours again if you don't come with me right now."

"Never," Amber said.

The bartender was continuing to force Johnny out of the lounge, when Johnny pushed his weight forward and threw the young man over his shoulder. He landed on his back with a loud thump and lay perfectly still on the floor.

Amber's gaze met Clint's for a second. She smiled at her son still in Clint's arms then looked back at Clint again. The bartender groaned, rolled over and grabbed Johnny's ankle. Amber mouthed the words thank-you to Clint. Johnny shook his foot but the bartender hung on. "I'm going to get you and that filthy kid," Johnny shouted.

Amber took another look at her pimp, spun on her heel and ran out the fire door. Johnny kicked the bartender and chased after her. Clint hated to think how Johnny would hurt Amber when he caught up with her—and he had no doubt he would. The bad guys always won in Amber's world. He started forward when the baby in his arms cried out in alarm.

Clint stopped dead in his tracks. He needed to help Amber but he couldn't abandon her child. He was about to give the child to the bartender when Laura walked in, looking cool and fresh in an ivory colored linen dress, her porcelain skin highlighted with a pretty pink in her cheeks. When she saw him holding the baby her blue eyes widened in surprise and she unsuccessfully tried to repress a smile.

She walked toward him. "I have to admit I never know what you'll be up to next. I never thought you'd try to pull attention away from Sweetums with a baby!"

"Don't be ridiculous," he growled and felt a muscle twitching near the corner of his mouth. "Here," he passed the child over to Laura, who clutched it tightly to her, looking like she was afraid to drop it.

"What do you want me to do with it?" She held the child away from her and looked at it with puzzlement. "Whose baby is this?"

"Look after it, I need to help someone." The baby let out a loud scream and started flailing its arms about. "It's not a bag of potatoes, hold the baby closer to you." He positioned Laura's arms so that she was nestling the child's head against her left breast, much like Amber had been holding the child earlier.

Laura's perfume was roses and something else, something that was feminine, uniquely Laura. He stepped away and cleared his senses. "Look after the child, I have to go after someone."

"Clint, wait. You can't leave me with a...a baby!" she called out to his retreating back, unable to believe that Clint Marshall left her holding the baby.

No one had ever given her a baby to hold, not even at one of her family's baby showers for the latest properly pregnant Carter. Not that she had attended all that many showers—first she'd been away at college, then at the police academy and then concentrating on her career—but every once in a while she gave in to her mother's demands and made an appearance. At the last shower, she and cousin Beverly had gamely struggled through a conversation until the disaster. Beverly had had her ten-month-old baby with her and had asked Laura to look after Junior. But as soon as the child's mother had left the room, Junior had begun to scream at the top of his lungs until one of the other women had taken him out of her arms. The child had immediately stopped screaming and had actually gurgled happily at the woman who'd rescued him. Laura had remained in her uncomfortable chair, humiliated.

What if it happened again? She looked at the child in horror. The baby looked back at her with equal surprise and made a funny face. "No, please don't cry. I'll buy you a car when you're sixteen if you don't cry."

The baby considered her words and blew a bubble. She laughed in surprise and the baby giggled as well. "You're a good baby, aren't you?" and then wondered whether she was holding a boy or girl. The baby's large blue eyes smiled back at her and she noticed the blue romper suit with figures of baseball players and deduced she was holding a boy. "Brilliant police work, Carter," she mocked herself.

"You're a great big strong man, aren't you?" she cooed. Perhaps this parenting thing was a little easier than she'd believed—and then recalled her own mother and shook her head. The baby boy blinked at her and she noticed his eyelashes were long like Clint's. She gasped. Was the baby his child? It couldn't be.

Why not? Clint was a virile attractive man. She'd seen a lot of women at the police station make their play for him. But why would Clint bring a baby on the assignment?

No, Clint was the big-hero type, he wouldn't endanger a small child. Clint took his Texas roots seriously.

So why was she standing in the lounge of the hotel bar holding a baby? She looked around and saw the room was deserted except for the bartender who was holding an ice pack against his jaw and speaking into a phone. "No need for security. Someone ran out the fire door." He hung up the phone. "We had to disconnect the sound on that damned door because two or three cheating spouses escape through it every month," he explained. "I have to call security and tell them it's nothing within thirty seconds or else the fire department will be here." He groaned as he pressed the ice pack to a different spot on his face.

"What happened?" she asked him.

"I should never get involved. I've been tending bar for three years and still I keep sticking my nose into other people's business."

"But what happened?" Laura repeated.

"Your friend was talking to a hooker when her pimp came in and threatened the two of them. Before we knew what was happening she took off, the pimp took off after her, leaving your friend holding the baby. And now you're holding the baby. Want a drink?"

"Er, no, I shouldn't while I have the baby," she replied rather inanely. Were the rules about holding a baby the same as driving a car? Were there rules about babies? She knew not to leave one alone in a bathtub, or put the baby car seat in the front seat of the car, but that was the extent of her knowledge.

The bartender poured whiskey into a glass and threw back a shot. "I needed that. Oh, no." He paled looking at something over her shoulder and then reached for the telephone under the bar.

Laura turned to see a disgusting looking, greasy haired man advancing toward her.

"Give me that kid," he said. He opened his arms as if he believed she would hand over the child to him.

She clutched the baby closer to her. "Call the police," she said to the bartender.

"I've called hotel security," the bartender shouted. "They'll be here in a minute. I suggest you leave before they get here."

Laura surveyed the man from head to toe in her best Carter family "I think I've smelled something nasty" raised-nose look. The disgusting man came closer and smiled, showing off a gold tooth. "That's my son. I'll take him now."

"No."

The man only smiled more broadly, his gold tooth flashing in the light. "Don't be crazy, lady. Give me the boy." He held out his arms and Laura stepped back. He kept moving forward as Laura retreated and hit the back of the bar. Her actions were severely limited by holding on to the baby. The pimp crowded in, placing his arms on the bar trapping her between them. "A pretty woman like you doesn't want to get hurt. Give me the kid."

The baby protested the disgusting man's smell and Laura raised her chin. "Would you please step away from me. I am not giving you this child so you might as well leave."

He showed even more teeth in a feral smile and moved his hands to Laura's shoulders.

"Let go of me, I don't want to hurt you."

He laughed and Laura raised her knee sharply, hitting him hard in the groin. He dropped to his knees with a scream. She shifted the child so that she was holding him firmly with one arm and with the other she grabbed hold of one of the man's many neck chains and tightened it like a garrote until his screams stopped. He had one hand clutching his privates while his other clawed furiously at the chain around his neck. Her technique might not be proper police procedure but it was effective.

Laura let go of the necklace and the man fell back.

"Leave me and my child alone." She kissed the top of the little boy's head and felt her knees shaking.

"Wow," the bartender said. "That was really cool. I called 9-1-1. The police will be here soon."

The man raised his head and she noticed an ugly purple mark across his throat. "I'll get you for this, bitch."

"Such language in front of the baby. Mind your manners."

He lurched to his feet and took a step toward Laura. She raised a brow. "I don't want to have to hurt you again," she repeated and let her gaze fall to his groin.

"I'd listen to what the lady says, she seems serious," a man's voice joined in. Laura turned her head to see Peter Monroe. The disgusting man lurched to his feet and began to edge out of the lounge.

"Should I stop him?" Peter asked, moving slightly so that he could block the man's path, his face steady and determined.

Laura didn't want a civilian to get involved, but she also didn't want to reveal she was a cop to Monroe. "He's dangerous," she said. "Let him leave. The police are bound to catch up with him outside the hotel."

As soon as she finished speaking, two uniformed police officers and three members of the Regal's security rushed in with Clint right behind them. They nabbed Johnny and immediately cuffed him. There was a blur of activity as the uniforms wrote up their report. Peter Monroe took over with the baby as the two cops talked to Laura and Clint. Clint pulled one of the cops over to a corner to identify himself as an undercover officer so the paperwork could proceed more smoothly. When he came back to stand next to her, Laura whispered, "What about the baby's mother? Did you find her?"

"No."

"What about the baby? We should turn it over to the cops."

"No," Clint had raised his voice and several people looked at him. "Amber is a working girl. She knows how to take care of herself. She'll get in touch with me soon. If we hand her child over to the authorities she'll have a hard time getting him back."

"Maybe it would be better for the child if he wasn't returned to his mother."

Clint looked at her, his mouth a thin line. "You sure are cold, Carter. The boy belongs with his mother. She loves him."

"And she put him into danger."

"Amber is trying to get out of the life," Clint insisted.

"We've both heard that story too many times to believe it."

"I believe her. I saw her face when she looked at her child. Now that Johnny is going to jail for threatening you—and some other charges I'm sure the DA will be able to think of—Amber will get the chance to change her life. Maybe move somewhere else. We're keeping the child until she comes for him." He glared at her, daring her to defy him.

Laura shook her head, "I hope you know what you're getting yourself into."

Clint nodded. "You did good before—with Johnny. The bartender said you took him down in about two seconds while still holding on to the child."

"I was good at self-defense in the police academy, although I'd never had to do it holding a baby before. How did you know Johnny was back in the bar?"

"When I lost Amber on the street I rushed back here. I saw what was happening, and that you had the situation temporarily under control when our backup arrived."

"Peter seemed very impressed." She looked across the room to where Peter was cooing to the child. He was studying the child with the same adoration he lavished on his wife. "What's the baby's name?"

Clint looked puzzled for a moment and then sheepish. "Um, Amber never mentioned it."

"You were looking at her baby, talking about her baby and you never asked his name?" The man wouldn't last a second at a baby shower.

"It never came up. How do you know it's a boy?"

"He's dressed in boy's clothes, it didn't take a great detective to figure that one out." She was thinking about what Clint had said about them needing something memorable to make their connection with Peter Monroe. He hadn't been impressed with their cowboy-and-heiress routine, but he was delighted with the child in his arms. A crazy idea began to form, but she pushed it back. Still... "Should we let Peter think the baby is ours?"

"What?" Clint asked horrified. "We can't pretend to be the baby's parents."

She nodded toward Peter. "Look at him with the child. It's the first time he's shown any interest in us despite the fact that we fit his psychological fantasy profile."

"I don't think the head guys really have this psychological fantasy business worked out."

"I agree. But look at Peter with the baby."

The multimillionaire was pretending to eat the baby's chubby fist, much to the howls of delight issuing from the little tyke.

"He's got some set of lungs," Clint agreed. "You're right. I was just thinking that we needed something dramatic for Peter to want to become friends with us. I guess the baby is it."

"And when Amber picks him up—later today?" she

added on hopefully. "What do we say about the baby when he disappears?"

"We'll tell everyone the baby-sitter came for him. She's had an emergency, which is why the child is with us now."

"Good plan," she agreed and looped her arm through Clint's. Together they walked over to Peter Monroe who smiled at them.

"You have a strong healthy son here—hopefully he'll turn out to be half as resourceful as his mother. You were very brave today."

"I couldn't let anyone hurt my baby," Laura said with conviction. "That man was deranged."

Peter shook his head as he handed the baby back to Laura. She took the child without flinching and while the baby looked back longingly toward Peter he settled into her arms without complaint.

"It looks like you have a fan," she told Peter as the baby continued to watch him.

He grinned broadly. "I love children. My wife and I haven't been lucky so far but we're thinking of adopting." He chucked the baby under the chin and then turned more serious. "Did the police say why they thought that man was after your child? I know an excellent private security firm I could recommend if you would like some extra protection. I'm also going to have a word with the management about their security. Their men were very careless."

"Thank you, but that's not necessary. The police think he needed money for drugs and thought that grabbing a child would be a quick way to get money from us," Clint informed him. "We sure do appreciate your assistance. It reminds me of the folks from back home."

"Where are you from?" Peter asked and Laura realized

that he was finally becoming interested in them as people—a couple who fit his fantasy profile.

"Two Horse Junction, Texas," Clint answered with his very best Texas twang.

"A fine state, Texas," Peter agreed and then his attention returned back to the baby.

"What's your son's name?"

Clint's mouth fell open a little and looked to Laura for help. *Really, men could be of no use when the answer was staring clearly at both of them,* she thought. It was her feminine instincts and not her police training telling her exactly how she and Clint could be bosom buddies with Peter Monroe.

She looked at the baby and then smiled brightly at the two men. "Peter. Our son's name is Peter."

4

"PETER. YOU HAD TO NAME the baby Peter?" Clint scowled at Laura, while she questioned her impulsive decision silently. She wasn't about to admit a second of doubt to Clint. The cowboy would use any weakness against her.

"Didn't you see how Monroe's face lit up when he realized the little boy was his namesake?" Laura felt her insides do a curious looping movement as she thought of Baby Peter. She straightened her back as she met Clint's thunderous expression. "The only thing that Peter Monroe has liked about us is our child, so I decided to expand on the fantasy a little."

"This is the craziest situation I've ever been in. And the stupidest. I can't believe that you, of all people, decided to pretend that we have a child." He paced away from her to the other side of the elevator and then turned to face her, his eyes glinting cold steel. "How do you even know the child will answer to Peter?"

"Need I remind you that *you* didn't even bother to find out his name." Laura pushed the elevator button again hoping it would speed up and take them to their dinner engagement with Peter Monroe and his wife, unwilling to admit she had doubts about what they were doing. What did he mean by his words: you, of all people? Did he think she lacked the imagination to improvise during an undercover situation? Or did he think she would make a terrible mother?

She stopped her thoughts. It should not, it *did* not matter to her what Clint Marshall thought of her. *Liar.* "It got us invited to dinner, didn't it?"

"Are you sure Petey will be okay with the hotel babysitter?"

"I checked her references, besides she knows more about taking care of a child than either of us do."

Clint raked a hand through his dark hair and Laura wished she didn't notice how dark and rich the color was, or the way one lock always fell forward making her itch to brush it back. If a woman kissed him she could run her fingers through his hair. Stop it, she told herself angrily. She was trapped together with Clint Marshall, the over-confident arrogant cowboy, for days so she needed to control her sexual fantasies—or she'd be pressing the Stop button of the elevator and ravishing him. She wondered if he'd ever done it in an elevator.

Probably. He was exactly the kind of man who would be overcome with lust for a woman and take her against the wall of an elevator.

Laura licked her suddenly dry lips and Clint scowled at her. "Why are you looking at me like that?"

She looked down at her shoes. Keep yourself together, Carter, she told herself. You've survived twenty-seven years of your family. You can survive a few days with an oversexed cowboy without revealing any of your feelings. She glared at him. "You left me alone with the baby for the entire afternoon. What were you thinking?" Despite her anxieties, Laura had enjoyed playing with the child but she wasn't about to let Clint know that.

"I went to look for Amber."

"Well you should have told me where you were going. In case you've forgotten we're supposed to be partners on this assignment. Equal partners. I'm not here just because I know how to wear the right clothes."

Which was the absolutely wrong thing to say because Clint's eyes ran over her body from head to foot leaving every inch of her tingling in response. He smiled his wicked slow cowboy smile and she grabbed the back of the elevator rail to keep herself upright. She pinched herself hard.

"If there's one thing we have to agree on it's that you sure do know how to dress...right." He said the last word on a suggestive whisper and she pinched herself even harder.

Luckily the elevator stopped and the doors opened and she hurried off, heading toward the restaurant. Clint's long strides had him caught up with her in a few steps. He looped his arm around her shoulders and she stopped herself from shivering.

Laura told herself it was lucky that the elevator doors had opened and Clint Marshall hadn't kissed her or done anything else—if he kissed her he'd know how much she wanted him. And she, Laura Carter of the Boston Carters, did not give in to weakness like her insane lust for the cowboy. This was just a test—one she would pass. A couple more days in his annoying company and she would lose all attraction to Clint.

They'd been together for over twenty-four hours and her attraction hadn't lessened, in fact it had increased, but more time would surely point out Clint's faults. His annoying habits would surface.

Peter Monroe and his wife were already waiting for them at their table. Peter stood as they approached and Laura noticed a small embroidered rose on his lapel in the same dark shade of blue as his suit and instantly recognized the exclusive London tailor her uncle Alfred favored. "I see Richard Longworth is still making your suits. I thought he had retired."

Peter's eyebrows raised. "He did retire but I convince him to make me a couple of suits every year."

Clint held out Laura's chair for her. "How lovely," she said as she sat down. "My uncle Alfred will be jealous. He swore by Longworth's tailoring."

"Where is your family from?" Peter asked.

"Boston. My mother is Veronica Ashworth and my father was Thomas Carter."

Peter raised an eyebrow. "The banking family?"

"Yes, but I'm afraid mother's family always treated him like a gigolo—despite his family's money." While the Ashworths hadn't come over on the *Mayflower*, they had only been a generation behind and had made their fortunes off the backs of the generations of immigrants that had come after them. Even though the Carter family had society roots back to the 1850s, the Ashworths considered them monied interlopers. After her mother's fifth marriage she'd reclaimed her maiden name. Laura remembered her words: "Ashworth really was the best family name I ever had, dear. And I've had so many of the good Boston family names. I don't know whatever possessed me to change it." She'd considered Laura. "You could legally change your name as well. Carter is so, well, common."

"I like Carter," she'd announced. In fact, she was proud of her surname because it sounded so ordinary. People didn't immediately know she was part of the Ashworths of Boston—the produce millionaires. If canned vegetables were on the menu, there was a good chance the Ashworth family owned the farm that had grown them, the canning plant and the distribution system.

But now in the most ridiculous case of her police career,

she was deliberately using her mother's name and connections and money. How ironic that after years of fighting to prove herself, her chance was due to the fact that she was an Ashworth. She needed her family. Well, just this once. And then it was back to being alone—Laura standing on her own two feet and not owing anyone.

Cassandra Monroe lowered her wineglass and stared at Laura. "Well my heavens, isn't Peter going to love you—the pair of you, in fact. My husband is obsessed with old money."

Peter took his wife's hand and raised it to his lips, brushing a kiss over her knuckles. "Dear, you exaggerate." He sat back and shrugged. "I have to admit a fondness for the *Mayflower* families, or any American who can trace his roots back for almost ten generations. I can't trace my roots back further than my grandparents so I take pleasure out of those families who have established traditions."

"Well then I hope you and Cassandra begin some family traditions very soon." Clint raised his glass and saluted them.

Laura kept her expression cool and collected, as she raised her glass in a toast as well and considered Peter's words. As a self-made man he had no idea how stifling family traditions could be. Nothing she had ever done had been good enough for her mother.

When Laura had announced she was going to become a police officer her mother had threatened to disown her. And then there had been Uncle Alfred's meddling in her job. She glanced at Clint and thought that whoever his family was, they never tried to ruin his life back in that Two Horse place he called home. Laura saw the others looking at her and realized she was frowning.

Cassandra smiled and pushed back a strand of raven-black hair. "You and your husband obviously come from such different backgrounds. You'll have to forgive my nosiness, but how did you and your husband meet?"

Laura felt Clint take hold of her hand and could only watch in a kind of fascinated horror—much like a traffic accident as it was happening—as he raised it to his lips and, copying Peter's actions, brushed a kiss across her knuckles. Her toes curled in her shoes. *Breathe*, she reminded herself.

He gazed at her adoringly and then turned to Cassandra. A lock of dark hair had fallen forward once again and Laura resisted her impulse to brush it off his face.

"It was on a cruise of all places," he began, his eyes warm and friendly as he answered Cassandra's question. Laura wished he'd look at her in the same melting manner. "I'd been thrown from a bull at the rodeo, being a darn fool and showing off. My doctor suggested I take a holiday to recuperate so I took my mother on a cruise— she'd always wanted to go. At dinner we had the good luck to be seated at the same table as Laura. I knew the moment I saw this beautiful filly she was the woman for me." He leaned in closer—he was going to kiss her, here, in front of everyone—and Laura shifted her head slightly so he brushed her cheek.

She took his hand, which had begun toying with a strand of hair that had come loose from the knot of hair she'd twisted on top of her hair, and squeezed it, hard. She gazed at him with something she hoped passed for adoration. "It took a little longer for me to fall for this guy."

"She had me chasing her all over that boat before she'd even look at me, much less kiss me."

His warm breath brushed her neck and she tingled. All over. She put his hand on the table hoping he would take the hint and stop touching her. "Ship, darling."

"Right." He shrugged. "A fellow with a few thousand acres doesn't know much about boats—ships. Anyway I wooed and won her. We were engaged by the end of the cruise."

"It was fast, but he just swept me off my feet!" Laura said in awe at the man's guile. "And now we divide our time between Clint's ranch in Texas and the family home in Boston. As long as I have Clint and little Petey any place is home."

"How romantic," Cassandra exclaimed and patted her husband's hand. "I'm afraid our story isn't nearly as romantic. Peter was buying Daddy's company when we met."

"She was the best part of the deal," Peter said his eyes softening as he looked at his wife.

She smiled at him but the warmth didn't extend to her eyes, and Laura realized she'd found a weak link in Peter Monroe's armor. His wife didn't like being a trophy. Cassandra had moved from being the daughter of a successful businessman to being the wife of one.

Laura decided to cozy up to Cassandra and use their shared experience of being judged because of their family instead of themselves. She just might learn something about Peter's business compatriots. She'd bet a year's worth of facials that Cassandra Monroe knew a lot more about Peter's business than he thought she did.

A bored woman would know a lot about her husband's business associates—and certainly have noticed any foreign associates. Cassandra could very well have the names that Garrow wanted, and be able to send Laura in the right direction as to how the money was being diverted through so many different divisions of his company.

Last year on an insurance fraud case, she'd concentrated on their main suspect's wife. The woman had reminded Laura of one of her mother's friends, and the fact that Laura had expressed interest in her life had made the woman talk and talk until she revealed that her husband was having an affair. The mistress knew where the husband's money was. Case closed.

Since she knew she wouldn't be able to sleep with Clint asleep in the living area of their suite, she'd use tonight's tossing and turning as a chance to plan how to get close to Cassandra Monroe. It would stop her from wondering about the impossibly sexy man in the room next to her. Wondering if he slept naked. Wondering what he would do if she slipped between the sheets next to him.

She knew what he would do. Clint Marshall didn't like her. He'd be polite and graciously make light of her attempted seduction and send her away with an *aw shucks* grin. A cowboy gentleman.

Being assigned to the sexy cowboy was more than frustrating. Every time Clint touched her she had the overwhelming urge to let herself sink into him. She stiffened her backbone and resolved to let no one know how the cowboy affected her—except of course when she was supposed to play the part of the loving wife.

The waiter arrived to take their orders and as Peter studied the wine list Laura took the opportunity to begin her new line of attack: Cassandra. "Peter must have swept you off your feet."

Cassandra took a sip of water. "Yes, he was very charming. He wined and dined Father and myself and almost before I knew it he had bought Father's company and I had agreed to marry him."

"Darling, it was more romantic than that." Peter protested. "I have to admit after I met Cassandra the business deal became purely secondary."

Cassandra smiled at him, but again Laura was aware there were currents underneath. From the besotted way Peter was looking at his wife she didn't think he felt the same doubts or frustrations his wife did.

The waiter arrived with their wine, uncorking it with a flourish. Peter pointed to his wife. "Let Cassandra try it, her taste is much better than mine."

"You do flatter me, dear." She tasted the wine and indicated her approval. Peter began asking Clint questions about his ranch and after a few minutes of talk about horses and cows, Laura turned to Cassandra who had a slightly glazed expression in her eyes.

"You'll have to forgive Clint, he does love to talk about his ranch. Or rather, he loves to talk about Texas." She shrugged.

Cassandra smiled genuinely. "Then he's found the right man in Peter. I keep expecting him to come home and announce he's bought Montana. Do you like Texas?"

Would she like a place like Texas? Laura couldn't imagine it. Wide open spaces and horses and cows. But what if all the men were virile specimens like Clint? Okay, so he was sexy and big but that wasn't what she wanted. Her attraction to him was just an aberration. She would soon have herself under control again.

"I like it because Clint likes it," she answered.

"Spoken like the true corporate wife," Cassandra said dryly.

"You chose to be a corporate wife," Laura probed.

The other woman took another sip of her wine. "That's true. I guess I thought with Peter I would have a little more freedom since he's a self-made man. I respect my husband very much because of how much he's accomplished, but..."

"But it's hard sometimes to know who you are," Laura finished for her.

Surprise crossed Cassandra's face. "Exactly."

"Lots of women in my family experience that exact problem all the time." Too many of them.

"Maybe if I came from that background all my life, but daddy only became rich when I finished college. I was used to being liked for myself."

"Of course, you're beautiful and smart."

Cassandra finished her wine. "Thank you."

"I'm sure your husband knows that as well."

She shrugged again. "I know he loves me, but after he won me he seemed to lose some of his interest."

Laura had seen it happen countless times, including in her mother's numerous marriages. Of course, her mother had always lost interest pretty quickly as well. "Couldn't you do something that would make you feel more...more..." she floundered for the right words.

"More, exactly." Something across the room caught the other woman's eyes. Laura looked to see the soon-to-be-newlywed couple step on to the dance floor and into each others arms. The young bride and groom floated around the room, aware only of each other. Cassandra sighed and Laura suppressed an urge to join in. She was supposed to be blissfully married. Out of the corner of her eye she noticed Clint give her a funny look. She ignored him.

"I think we could be friends," the beautiful wife said, "You're one of the few people who seems to know what I'm talking about."

"My mother has been married many times. I vowed I wasn't going to repeat her mistakes," Laura said honestly aware too late that Clint was now listening to their conversation.

The band stopped playing and the band leader took the

microphone. "I'd like to dedicate this dance to the future Mr. and Mrs. Kyle Chandler—and everyone else who's in love tonight."

The band swept into a waltz as the room—most of them wedding guests—applauded. Peter raised his glass. "To love."

Cassandra was watching the young couple as she sipped her wine. "They're so much in love, how romantic. How do you know the newlyweds?"

"We barely do," Laura admitted. "When my mother realized Kyle Chandler—he's the son of one of her childhood friends—was getting married she insisted we had to attend all the festivities to represent the family. I'm afraid we were a rather last-minute addition to the guest list."

"In Texas it's nothing to have a few more people drop in on your wedding, but things are done a little different back East," Clint drawled. "Laura's mother was upset that she would be in London for the affair so we promised to attend in her place. Spending the weekend in a ritzy hotel with my wife seemed like a nice idea for another honey-moon. Although," he took her hand and brushed a kiss across her knuckles, "I don't think the first honey-moon has ever ended."

"We don't know a lot of the guests either," Peter admitted. "I've got some business dealings with the Chandlers and Cassandra wanted to shop so it seemed like a good idea to attend. Now that I've met the two of you, I'm very glad we did."

Laura realized that Clint had stood and held out his hand to her. "They're playing our song," he said, his voice soft and alluring.

Laura let herself be led out onto the dance floor and then swept into his arms. She felt enveloped by his body heat and presence even though he held her gently, one large hand low on the center of her back, the other holding her hand. The band was playing "What a Wonderful World."

"This is one of my favorite songs," she said.

"It's beautiful," he said, "and so are you."

Laura knew she was blushing and cursed her fair countenance.

"We could always make this our song for real," he said and twirled her. When Laura regained her composure she saw Clint laughing at her. He was playing with her. Through the red haze of anger and embarrassment, she noticed Peter and Cassandra had also joined on the dance floor and realized that Clint was putting on a show for their mark.

Well, two could play at that game. As she settled back into his arms she moved in a little closer so that her body pressed intimately against his. He inhaled sharply but the teasing look on his face didn't change. "Are you having a good time?" he asked.

She took her hand off his muscular shoulder and brushed the lock of dark hair off his forehead. She let her fingers run through his thick hair, tracing a finger around the outside of his left ear. A muscle twitched by the side of his mouth.

"What are you doing?" he asked between clenched teeth. The well-practiced adoring smile remained on his face.

She widened her eyes slightly and missed a step so that their hips bumped. She looked over at the Monroes and saw that Peter was watching them. She smiled brilliantly at Clint. "Why, playing the part of the loving wife. Cassandra doesn't seem quite as infatuated with Peter as he is with her."

Clint's gaze turned serious. "Good work. Maybe you

can spend some time with her tomorrow. She might be our in to Peter's operation."

"Whatever that is," she returned with frustration at this crazy case. She was beginning to think more and more that she and Clint were on a wild-goose chase. She looked at the Monroes again and saw Cassandra studying the two of them. She raised herself on her toes and brushed a kiss along the side of Clint's mouth and then pressed her cheek against his, whispering into his ear. "They're watching us."

Clint had stiffened when her lips first touched his—did he really find her so unappealing?—but then he relaxed, using the hand on her back to pull her more closely against him. Her body fit perfectly against his and she inhaled deeply of his woodsy, masculine scent. Earlier she had meant to use this dance as a chance to tease Clint a little, but now she realized she wanted this opportunity to taste him, to discover the texture of his skin. She moved her head slightly and nibbled his ear. *Mmm he tastes wonderful*, she thought as he missed a step.

"What are you doing?" Clint demanded.

"Quiet," she whispered against his ear and then blew very softly into it. She was gratified by the way his hand against her back clenched. But it wasn't enough. Now that her lips had felt the hard and soft texture of his skin she wanted more—and she had the coward's excuse to do exactly as she desired. She turned her head a little to the left so that she could brush light kisses along the side of his jaw.

Somehow their bodies had shifted so that one of Clint's legs was between her own and she pressed against it.

"Laura—" Clint gasped out.

"Sssh, they're watching us," she said, although she had no idea what anyone else on the dance floor was doing.

All she was aware of was what it felt like to be in Clint's arms. She licked the cleft in his chin and Clint stopped moving. Slowly she became aware that the music had stopped, but his dark eyes were gazing down at her with question and awareness and she didn't stop to think about what she was going to do next.

She raised herself on her tiptoes and she kissed him. She pressed her lips full and ravenously over his, not caring who might see them, what anyone, including Clint, might think. She had to kiss him. She had to know what it was like.

It was lovely and a whirlwind at the same time. Clint's arms wrapped around her, curving over her hips, squeezing gently to send liquid melting heat through the lower part of her body, pulling her off her feet to meet his kiss.

Because it was no longer her kiss.

And it wasn't his kiss either. It was the two of them locked together in a primal exploration. His lips pressed hard against her, testing and tasting.

She heard something low and guttural and realized it was Clint. She grabbed his hair and tugged pulling his mouth down to just how she wanted it on hers and when she got it her toes seriously curled. She was barely aware of the fact that one of her shoes fell off as his mouth continued to devour hers.

Her heart was pounding in her ears until she realized it wasn't the blood pounding through her body that she heard but applause.

Applause?

Like a bucket of cold water thrown on a pair of rutting farm animals Laura realized the rest of the restaurant was cheering on their amorous display.

She tore herself out of his arms. She did not lose control. Certainly no man had ever made her lose control.

Clint looked at her, his dark eyes filled with raw need as his arms moved up her back to press her closer to his, lowering his head for another kiss.

If she let him kiss her again, she would be lost. Using all of her Carter family backbone she straightened hers and raised a finger against his lips. He looked at her in shock as she pasted on a false smile. She wished she could just keep on kissing him, let them both proceed to where that kiss had been heading—the bedroom.

But her pride returned. She couldn't let Clint know that her kisses had been anything more than part of the assignment.

She cocked her head to one side, pointing to where Peter and his wife were sitting at their table. Peter had a big silly grin on his face.

"I think we've made our point," she said. "Peter Monroe now believes we are head over heels in love." She stepped away from him, needing the space so she could breathe in air that wasn't filled with Clint.

She smiled wickedly. "Although I must admit, if I had known that cowboys really did kiss as good as you, I would have visited Texas long ago."

She turned on her heel and headed back to their table leaving Clint staring after her. She felt the heat of his anger on her shoulders with every step she took away from him.

Don't fall in love with a cowboy, Laura recalled the lyrics to the song.

She planned to follow that advice faithfully. And after her behavior this evening, Clint was sure to despise her more than ever.

So why did that depress her?

5

A FEW HOURS LATER, after forcing down a meal he hadn't tasted, telling Peter Monroe tall tales about Texas and wondering how Laura could get under his skin so easily, Clint opened the door to their suite and a large powder puff attacked his legs. Perfect.

He scooped up Sweetums with one hand, "Careful, you're going to get caught under the heel of my boot." The dog ignored his words and began to lick his face and make a lot of curious excited noises and panting.

When he had finally come to his senses after being assaulted by Laura, he'd realized that they held the entire restaurant entranced by their public display. It was a good thing his mother had taught him to be a gentleman or he would have hauled Laura up over his shoulder and they would have finished what they had begun on the dance floor on that very big honeymoon bed in the next room.

Sweetums continued to lick excitedly at his face.

"Goodness, I've never seen her take to a stranger like she has to you." Laura entered their room and took Sweetums into her arms. The dog whined and twisted in Laura's arms looking for Clint. Laura held the dog to her face and shook her head disapprovingly. "You really are taken with the cowboy, aren't you, dear?"

Sweetums paid no mind and began a high-pitched whine. "Give her back to me," Clint said irritably. Laura passed the bundle of fluff over to him, her clear blue eyes shining with amusement.

"This isn't funny," he said, annoyed at how calm and collected she was—and had been ever since that kiss on the dance floor.

The kiss on the dance floor. He wasn't going to think about that right now.

Laura walked farther into the suite and he admired the smooth sway of her hips and how they filled out her dress. "I'm going to check on the baby and change my clothes. Then we should try to make some kind of plan for tomorrow. Peter may like the fact that you're a cowboy and we have an adorable son, but we haven't seen any examples of him wanting to compete against you like Garrow said he would. Maybe we can come up with a better idea than what the psychologist suggested."

"Do you really think we can learn anything that Garrow hasn't uncovered in almost two years of investigation?" Clint asked.

"We have little Petey—he's our trump card. My instincts tell me that he's going to bring us closer to Monroe."

The hotel baby-sitter came out of the bedroom holding out her chit for Clint to sign. He scrawled his signature wondering how he was going to explain baby-sitting services in his expense report, then opened his wallet to tip the young woman. After the woman had left Clint felt his feet begin to follow Laura into the honeymoon bedroom. He stopped himself. Her words had not been an invitation. Just as the kiss—passionate kisses—hadn't been an invitation. She had been coolly amused when she'd spoken to him after the kiss. Her pretend passion had all been part of their assignment.

He didn't even like her very much, he reminded himself.

Liking the women he slept with was very important to Clint. Unlike his father who had chased any and everything that walked in a skirt, Clint took the relations between men and women very seriously.

Laura Carter was not the kind of woman he liked. She was too uptight, she never let down her defenses, or joined in with her fellow officers for a good time. Indeed he was almost surprised she owned a dog. Even a silly fluffball like Sweetums. As if she knew that he was thinking unkindly about her, Sweetums growled in her throat and chewed on one of Clint's fingers.

"Petey's asleep. I never realized how angelic babies look when they're sleeping." Laura came back into the living room, reaching behind her for the zipper of her dress.

"That's because he's not crying."

"Do you want the bedroom tonight? We could alternate nights. Darn, this zipper always gets stuck. Could you help?" she asked pivoting to give him access to the zipper.

"Sure," he said and moved toward her too aware that she stood at the threshold of the honeymoon bedroom. Surely she had no idea of the seductive image she made holding her blond hair above her neck, her back slightly arched as she waited for him to help her lower the zipper. He took a deep breath which was a mistake as he breathed in her unique scent. Reminding himself again that his mother had raised a gentleman, that he was on assignment, he pulled the zipper down exposing a long length of soft lily-white skin and the beige lace of her bra. A quick glance down her bare back assured him that her panties matched the lace of her bra. He raised a finger unable to resist the temptation of touching her when Laura jumped away from him.

She whirled around, her cheeks pink. "Thank you, I can manage on my own now."

He took a step closer to her. "Why did you kiss me?" He moved in until they were only inches apart. Laura raised her chin, her blue eyes wide and fresh. How could any woman be as fresh and appealing as her? Her unzipped dress slipped off one shoulder and Clint reached out to place it back, letting his finger linger too long on the top of her shoulder.

"Kissing you is part of the assignment," she said, her voice soft and breathy. Her lipstick had worn off and the natural soft rose color of her lips tempted him. He wanted to kiss her again.

He moved in a little closer, and her blue eyes widened. "What assignment?" he asked.

"Our stupid assignment," she whispered. "Connecting Peter Monroe to the money. What are you... Stop touching me like that."

He continued tracing a circle on the top of her shoulder. "You have very soft skin."

"There's no one here to impress with your routine." She didn't move away from him but continued to watch him watch her.

"I know."

"I don't fall for your cowboy act."

"Not even a little?"

"I've seen the way the women at the station house throw themselves at you. I'm not like that."

"Did you ever see me chasing after any of them?"

"That's because you probably have a stable of them at home."

"I live in an apartment. There's no room to have a stable."

"Oh," she said very quietly as he lowered his mouth to

hers until a kiss was only milliseconds away, wondering if she would break away. Instead her lips parted on a gasp of breath he moved to capture when a loud rapping sounded at the door. Clint swore. He let go of her and strode over to it. "Who is it?"

"Room service."

He looked back at Laura and she shook her head. He was going to get rid of this guy and kiss Laura before she changed her mind and he died from need. "We didn't order room service."

"I have champagne, compliments of the hotel," the voice from the other side of the door insisted.

Champagne. They could have some after they'd slaked their thirst in other ways first. If it really was a bellboy.

Clint pulled out his gun in case one of Johnny's cronies had found them and was after the child. He stood on one side of the entry. "Just leave it outside the door," he shouted, ready to spring it open and grab the man on the other side as soon as he heard the man make a move.

"Just open the door," the voice on the other side pleaded.

Clint frowned. Laura moved into position opposite him. In one quick move he twisted the knob, opened the hotel door and pulled the man into their room. Laura slammed the door shut as Clint jammed his gun into the throat of the bellboy. Clint let the gun press against the man's Adam's apple for a moment and then released him, finally recognizing Agent Garrow.

"What are you doing here?" Laura demanded. She put her gun on top of the bar and shimmied about in her dress—Clint realized she was zipping it back up.

Garrow rubbed his neck and cleared his throat. "I told you I would be in contact. I'm making contact."

"We didn't expect you to show up as our bellboy."

"Have you learned anything?"

Laura moved across the room and sat down on the blue-and-gold striped couch. She tucked one leg behind her and her dress raised a couple of inches on her thighs. Clint frowned as he saw Garrow studying her legs. "We've only been on the case for a day. Your team has been investigating Peter Monroe for months."

"You've only got three days before the wedding."

"Yes, and in that time you expect us to get a confession out of Monroe?"

Garrow shrugged. "Now that Vasili will be attending the wedding as well, I'm convinced there's a chance you really might find something."

"As long as you don't mess up our operation," Clint said. And then, to his horror, he heard the baby cry. Laura shot a nervous look toward their bedroom, jumped to her feet and took a step toward the room. Clint waved her back—they couldn't let Garrow know about the infant.

Garrow might consider them his last best chance to close the case on Peter Monroe, but he was still a special agent. He played the operation by the book; he would not let them keep Amber's baby.

"What's that?" Garrow looked toward the bedroom and then at the two of them.

"It sounds like a baby," Laura answered. "It's shocking how thin walls can be even in a good hotel like this one."

Garrow looked back at the large honeymoon bedroom. "I could swear it sounds like it's coming from in there."

Laura laughed, the sound deep and rich. "A baby, here? In the honeymoon suite? You do have a delightful sense of humor, Agent Garrow." She stepped next to him, turning slightly so that they were facing away from the bedroom and she touched Garrow's arm. "I don't think I thanked you for booking us into the honeymoon suite. I haven't stayed in such a luxurious room since mumsy and I went to Paris." She steered him toward the couch and leaned in confidentially. "Where do you usually stay?"

"When I'm in Paris?"

"Yes. Nothing really compares to the Ritz-Carlton Hotel, but I'm always willing to consider something new. Although convincing Mumsy to try a new place is a different story altogether. She believes in the tried-and-true—she calls them her classics."

Garrow blinked while Clint grinned at Laura's princess routine—her voice had tightened while her movements became more languid. She crossed her legs and touched Garrow on the arm.

"I've never been to Paris," he finally got out.

"What a shame. I'm sure you would love it. It's such a romantic city." She looked up at him from under her lashes. "Are you married, Agent Garrow?"

The man blushed, turning as red as the young clerk at the counter when Laura had flirted with him and convinced him to let Sweetums stay in the hotel. As if on cue, Sweetums ran out of the bedroom her pink bow flopping, heading straight toward Garrow carrying a squeaky toy in her mouth.

"What the heck?" Garrow asked.

Clint swooped the large dustball into his arms and swiftly took the baby's rattle out of the dog's mouth and pocketed it. "This is Laura's dog, Sweetums."

"A dog?" Garrow said. "That's against regulations. I'm not sure—"

Laura stood and pushed her hair behind her ears. "The dog fits my society image. Peter is quite convinced. I suggest you let me play the part you wanted. After all I am the expert." Her words were crisp and cold. She motioned toward the door. "Now that you've made sure we're all right, is there anything else you wanted to share with us?"

Garrow looked surprised to discover that Laura had walked him to the door. "Er, no."

"Well then fine, I'm glad we settled that." She smiled brilliantly. The baby had remained mercifully quiet after its one cry, but Clint wished Garrow out of the room as fast as possible. Peter Junior could make his presence felt at any second. The baby rattle felt like a loaded revolver in his pocket.

Laura had her hand on the doorknob, when another knock sounded. "Heavens, it's like Grand Central station in here." She stopped Garrow by holding on to his arm, tucking it closely against her. "Let me see who's at the door."

"Of course," Garrow answered but he didn't move away from Laura. Clint placed a hand on Garrow's shoulder and pulled him away from her.

"Who's there?" Laura called out.

"It's me, Peter Monroe."

Laura and Clint's eyes met and they both looked at Garrow. "I have to hide," he said.

"The other room," Clint pointed toward the bedroom but Laura shook her head.

"The closet." She grabbed Garrow's arm.

"I'll hide in the bedroom, there will be a lot more room."

"But you'll be able to hear so much better from the closet," she improvised and firmly but definitely dragged him to the closet, opened it and pushed him inside. "No matter what happens, be quiet."

The baby chose that inopportune moment to cry. Vince Garrow froze in the motion of pulling the door shut. "What was that?"

"Nothing. Now stay there until I tell you to come out."

Peter Junior cried louder.

"It sounds like a baby." Vince tried to look past her shoulder as she pushed on his shoulders, trying to stuff him back into the closet.

"Sssh," she said rather desperately when Garrow didn't move an inch. "Do you want Peter Monroe to see you?"

"No, of course not—he might recognize me. I worked for his organization for a couple of months, trying to find the information we needed to connect him to Vasili's money."

"Then hide."

"But—"

"I'll knock you out if you don't hide yourself," Clint said from behind Laura's shoulder as he shut the door on Garrow's protesting face.

"Thank goodness," Laura whispered. "I thought he was heading to the bedroom for sure."

"What do you think Peter Monroe wants with us now? After our public display on the dance floor, you'd think he'd think we were...er...busy."

"You're blushing." Laura looked at him with surprise. "That's sweet. Does that work on all your women?"

"What did I ever do to you to make you think so badly of me?"

"What did you do? You took one look at me and decided all the stories about me had to be true. And you said—"

He raised a brow in genuine curiosity. "What did I say?"

"We should answer the door."

He glared at her, mesmerized by how sharp her blue eyes had become. "What door?"

"The door Peter Monroe is behind—and wondering why we're not answering."

He snapped out of his brief sexual enchantment. He had completely forgotten the case, the fact that Garrow was hiding in the closet, that they had a fugitive baby in the honeymoon bedroom or that the target of their case was on the other side of the door. He was distracted by thoughts of how much he would like to make love to Laura in the honeymoon bedroom.

Laura moved past him toward the hallway door but he put his hand on her shoulder stopping her. "Now what?" she demanded.

"We look a little too tidy to have been interrupted doing what we were supposed to have been doing."

"Oh, right," Laura said and bit her lip.

He took off his bolero tie, undid the buttons on his shirt and pulled it free from his pants. "Muss up your hair and your lipstick," he suggested as Laura stared at him. He liked the way her eyes widened when she looked at his bare chest. She caught herself ogling him, turned her head upside down and ran her fingers through her hair. At the sight of her long blond hair, her long neck, he swallowed. She raised herself upright, her hair a big tangle all around her face and wiped the back of her hand across her mouth smudging what remained of her lipstick.

"Good," he said. "Now we look like we've been interrupted."

"We were. Just not doing what we were supposed to be doing." She grinned at him and he grinned back. "Come on, it's showtime."

Clint opened the door, an unexpected feeling of good humor washing over him. He'd never have guessed that working with Laura could at times be so pleasant—even with Garrow hiding in the closet and Peter Junior hidden in the bedroom.

On the other side of the door, Peter looked from Clint to Laura back to Clint again, taking in Clint's bare chest. Then he smiled broadly. "Still honeymooning. Good for you two. Nothing like keeping the romance alive in any relationship. Listen, since I've interrupted you anyway can I come in for a minute?"

"Of course," Laura said smoothly and indicated a chair in the living area of the suite.

"Excellent." He bounded in. For the first time Clint noticed he was holding a stuffed animal with a large blue bow. He held it out toward Clint. "It's a giraffe. For your son. Peter."

Clint took the stuffed toy and stared at it, unsure what a father would do at this point. As if she knew, Laura moved next to him, slipped an arm through his and lay her head against his shoulder. With her free hand she took the giraffe and held it eye level. "He's just the sweetest thing ever. Little Petey will love him. How did you know he was so fond of animals?"

"What kid isn't?" he asked disingenuously.

"This is truly so thoughtful of you," Laura continued. "Clint and I were saying earlier how we felt that we were making a real connection with you. The beginning of a genuine friendship if I'm not being too bold."

Peter bounced on his heels. "I knew I was being presumptuous coming back tonight but I felt the same way and wanted to invite you to come to the boat tomorrow. Cassandra and I are taking out the newlyweds and I thought you might like to come along. Lots of the young people are going on a cruise tomorrow, but Cassandra thought Kyle and Penelope might like to be with a smaller group. Prewedding jitters and all that." He turned to

Clint. "The way you described your horses, the passion and wonder you have for them. I feel the same way about my sailboat and want the chance to show off."

Clint's stomach lurched. Great, Peter was becoming competitive. But a boat...

"That would be marvelous. I haven't been out on a boat since we got married. Mother's second husband had a yacht, and then her fourth husband bought an even bigger one. He named it *Laura* after me. We had a lot of good times at that boat." She smiled tremulously and hooked her arm through his. "Let's go shall we, darling?"

Clint's stomach pitched again, but he quashed it down. "Anything you want, sweetheart."

"Thank you, you're the absolute best. I don't know how I ever got to be so lucky as to find you."

"Darlin', I'm the one who's lucky."

Little Petey cried from the other room clearly upset by all the cloying sweetness being spread around in the living room.

"I'll check on him," Laura said. "I'll take him the giraffe, he'll be delighted." She picked up the animal, smiled at Peter and headed to the bedroom. Clint and Peter watched her attractive backside leave the room.

"You're a very lucky man, Marshall."

"I know."

"I'm glad that her mother's five marriages didn't make Laura gun-shy about going to altar."

Clint realized that Peter had been checking out their backgrounds. Laura had been chosen specifically because of her family's prominence and Peter had bought it lock, stock and barrel. Now he was the one who didn't know anything about Laura's family. Her mother had been married five times? How did a child survive something like that?

Laura came back with baby Peter cradled in her arms. "He wanted to say thank-you for the giraffe. He's naming the giraffe Horace."

"That's a good old-fashioned name."

"It was my grandfather's. He died when I was very young."

Peter looked at the baby. "You know the real reason I came to your room was because I wanted to see your son again. He's very handsome."

"We love him a lot," she said. If he hadn't known better Clint would have said she was telling the truth.

"Well I'd better go. I've disturbed you two long enough." He chucked Peter Junior under the chin one last time. "I'll see you tomorrow."

"I'll just put Peter back to sleep," Laura added quickly, with a significant glance toward the closet where Garrow was hiding. Clint wondered how much the agent would be able to hear. If they were lucky this old hotel was well insulated. He doubted they would be that lucky and began to weave a story in his head about why they had a baby. Nothing he came up with sounded good even to himself.

Peter Monroe held out his hand and they shook solidly as if they were old friends. For the first time, Clint felt a twinge that he was deceiving this man. Peter was a criminal he reminded himself. This was his job.

He kept Peter Monroe at the door for a minute, giving Laura longer to settle the baby, but Peter now seemed anxious to leave, "I want to get back to Cassandra," he winked at Clint meaningfully. Clint kept the door open as Peter hurried down the hallway and disappeared into the elevator, until he felt Laura's presence behind him.

"He's gone?"

"Yes." Clint closed the door and both he and Laura

looked toward the closet with horrified fascination. The door opened immediately and Garrow stepped out, his eyebrows meeting as one furious black line across his forehead.

He cast them a scathing look before storming into the bedroom. Laura caught Clint's gaze and shrugged as they followed Garrow. Clint wondered what he thought he was doing when he'd decided to keep the baby for Amber. He should have called Social Services immediately.

At the least he would tell Garrow that keeping the baby had been his idea and he'd dragged Laura into it kicking and screaming.

Garrow stood in front of the baby's crib, looking like he'd smelled Peter Junior's diaper. "What is this?"

"It's a baby. He's named Petey," Laura answered firmly.

"Where did it come from?"

"It's my fault. I—"

"It's Clint's fault that the baby woke up" Laura interjected smoothly. "He was supposed to help me with him earlier but he stayed downstairs instead."

Garrow's face was red as he stared at the child like he was the criminal mastermind behind the money laundering. "Who's baby is this? Why do you have a baby on assignment?"

Laura put the pacifier in the baby's mouth and he stopped crying. "The baby was a stroke of genius, Clint's in fact. Nothing we did attracted the Monroes to us, I was beginning to think that your profile about him was all wrong. But as soon as Clint mentioned our baby, Monroe became very interested."

"But where did you get a baby from? We can't have a child in any danger."

"Of course not. What kind of people do you think we

are? Clint and I would never do anything that would endanger the baby." She stroked Petey's head.

"Of course not," Clint agreed, wondering where Laura
was going with this.

"I borrowed my girlfriend's baby for a couple of days.
She and her husband were planning to go away for the
weekend when her baby-sitter got sick and I stepped in.
Simple." She smiled.

"Simple," Clint agreed.

"Not so simple," Garrow said and then stumbled. "You
can't have a baby on the case."

"But the baby is what brought Peter here tonight to invite us to spend the day with him. If you want us to get
anywhere with this case, we need the baby. And we need
you." Laura smiled even more sweetly and Clint waited.

Garrow's shoulders stiffened. "Why do you need me?"

"Why to baby-sit, of course."

6

"I DON'T THINK Garrow had any idea what he was getting himself into when he agreed to baby-sit," Clint said as he studied the dock in front of him. Why would any reasonable person voluntarily want to spend several hours on a leaky boat?

"I don't think he actually agreed. We blackmailed him."

"You're being very accurate," he groused, looking for a loose board he could trip over and break a foot before he had to go aboard Monroe's boat. This morning was even worse than last night, which he'd spent most of awake staring at the ceiling, remembering the feel of Laura in his arms, the taste of her lips. She was so close, all he'd have to do was walk into the bedroom and...he shut down his thoughts. Laura Carter wasn't the kind of woman he wanted to be involved with, no matter the chemistry. Just because he was reacting to the role they were playing, to their close proximity, to her beauty, he didn't like her very much. He had to remember that.

His rationalizations hadn't made the night any more comfortable.

"It's a beautiful day and we're going sailing. I can afford to be generous." Laura smiled at him and he grimaced, momentarily distracted by her sheer joy. She linked her arm through his as they walked along the dock toward Monroe's vessel.

"Although I do feel a little guilty at leaving little Petey behind. I don't think babies make good sailors."

"They don't," Clint said firmly although he knew as little about babies as Laura. Still they'd had fun this morning trying to get Petey to eat and figuring out how to bathe him. Garrow had shaken his head when he'd seen the bathroom.

"Maybe we'll hit it lucky and his boat will be filled with incriminating documents," Laura added, practically skipping beside him.

"Yes, and under the influence of a glass of iced tea he'll tell us everything. Give us the secret codes and the numbers to his Swiss bank account."

"Exactly."

They walked along the docks to Pier 33 where the Monroe boat, the *Boston Belle* was launched. "*Boston Belle*," Clint drawled, "it could have been named after you."

She didn't let his words ruffle her, it was far too beautiful a day for that. "I haven't been sailing for years."

"Why not?"

"It was mother's fourth husband who was the real sailor. He taught me and we'd go out on most weekends, but then he and mother got divorced."

"But surely you had other friends who sailed."

"Yes, I did. It was part of my social set. But it was never as good as when Wayne and I went out. Afterwards I realized of course that I'd enjoyed having a father figure around, and it was the one thing he and I did together without mother. I had been hoping that mother would stay married to him."

"But she didn't," he said very quietly.

"No, she didn't. The women in my family don't have a very good track record with men. My grandmother buried two husbands, divorced one and ignored the last one. To her very great chagrin he outlived her and inherited some of her money."

"Did your mother lose a lot of her money to her husbands?"

"Every marriage cost her, but she hasn't learned her lesson."

"It sounds like they cost you even more."

She looked at him. "They did. The one thing I always promised myself is that I wouldn't become my mother—no matter what."

"That's why you became a cop?"

"Partly. Usually, in my family, the women take a nice, vaguely glamorous job. Maybe work in pubic relations or advertising. A couple of really ambitious cousins became lawyers and run their father's companies."

"But you decided to be a cop. Why?"

"I liked the idea of it—helping people. Justice. Retribution for those who've wronged you."

Clint understood her words completely. He was making up for his father's mistakes. He wondered if she had a similar motivation or if it was simply to get as far away as possible from her family. "Your family must have shuddered when you became a street cop."

"Worse." She stopped and Clint wondered if she would tell him. Finally she sighed. "They pretended it never happened."

"What?" He looked at her with disbelief.

"My mother never told anyone. That's why I didn't need to worry that anyone at this wedding might blow my cover. No one knows. My cousins assumed I was travelling or shopping or something. That's why Cassandra Monroe knows of my family but has no idea that I had become a cop. By the time her father got rich and she joined my social set, I was more or less out of it."

"So you became the black sheep of the family by becoming a cop."

"Yes." Laura spotted the soon-to-be-marrieds approaching the pier from the opposite direction and waved at them. The pair stopped and exchanged heated words, then noticing Clint and Laura staring at them waved back.

"It looks like the about-to-be-newlyweds are having cold feet," Clint said. What little he knew of Kyle Chandler and Penelope York came from their files—Garrow had conducted background checks on all the key players in the wedding. Chandler's family was well-established like Laura's, while Penelope's family were self-made millionaires, having made their money as down-market clothing manufacturers. This would be the first time he and Laura met the young couple face-to-face. He was curious about their family differences. Love could overcome a lot—but not what you wanted out of life. If Penelope and Kyle wanted the same kind of life they would be fine. But if they were like his mother and father, then they were doomed. His mother had loved Two Horse Junction and dreamed of raising a family and continuing her family's long history in the town. His father had been an adventurer who was always sure that the next best thing was waiting for him in the next town. While his parents had fallen deeply in love and married and had three sons, it hadn't been enough.

It was the same with him and Laura. Despite how soft her skin, or delectable her lips he wasn't going to kiss her or make love to her. The cowboy and the heiress. It was as ridiculous as it sounded.

The only thing they had in common was that she had as much to prove to her family as he had to prove to his hometown. Laura linked her arm through his and pushed back the blond hair that was blowing out of her ponytail.

"Do we have a plan for how we're going to get Peter Monroe to spill his guts?"

"Charm him. I'll do my very best cowboy and you, well just be yourself."

"The ice princess." The words were out of Laura's mouth before she could even think about them. Why did she actually tell Clint what she was thinking when she never revealed her thoughts to anyone else? He irritated her and confounded her in her own reactions to him. She had a crush on him—well more a full-fledged lust attack—but that shouldn't mean she also had to like him.

He was an irritation—one she didn't want to scratch no matter how bad or deep under the skin the desire went— and there was no reason for her to like him.

Clint stopped and because he was holding her arm she was forced to stop as well. She tried to tug free but he held on. Sighing she turned to face him. His gray eyes looked at her seriously, the usual mocking smile wiped off his face. "I should have known you'd hear me. I'm sorry."

"Sorry that I heard what you really thought?" she asked, suddenly defensive. "Don't worry, cowboy, your opinion doesn't mean anything to me."

Clint held her arm, his gaze holding hers captive. "I'm sorry I said it at all. You threw me for a loop when you first came into the department. You make one hell of a first impression, Princess, but you wouldn't give anyone the time of day. So it was easier to make fun of you then get to know you. I apologize."

Her cheeks burning, she pulled her arm free of his. She didn't want to hear any more about how Clint thought she was cold, stiff and uninterested in her fellow workers. "Fine, apology accepted. We should get onboard before everyone wonders what happened to us."

"Laura—" Laura had raced several steps ahead of him.

He didn't really know what more he would say to her. All he knew was that Laura Carter was becoming more and more intriguing. And he was beginning to think the only way to get over his curiosity for her—there were no other words to describe his fascination with her—was to take her to bed. A round or two of hot, sweaty sex—seeing just how hot and sweaty Ms. Laura Carter could get—would end this thing he had for her.

But first he had to live through a day on the *Boston Belle.* He looked at the forty-something-foot boat and cursed under his breath. His stomach lurched and he felt a bead of sweat break along his neck. He was not going to be seasick. It was simply a matter of mind over matter, or in this case of mind over water. A few little waves weren't going to defeat him.

Although he'd feel a lot better if Peter Monroe had wanted to pull on a pair of boots and saddle up a horse rather than deck shoes and the unpredictable water. "Think of it as a bucking bull, you've survived breaking in enough of those," he said out loud.

Laura turned back. Her calm, ice-princess exterior was back in place. "Did you say something?"

"Just admiring the boat."

"She's a beauty, isn't she?" Laura sighed with satisfaction. "This is going to be great. I can't imagine a better way to spend a more perfect day."

Far too quickly for his liking, Clint boarded the *Boston Belle,* shaking hands with Peter. Cassandra shouted hello from the back of the boat, where they made their way to deck chairs. Kyle and Penelope caught up with them, although from their flushed faces their disagreement was continuing.

As the introductions were made the bride and groom weren't surprised to meet more wedding guests they didn't know. "Gosh, there are so many people here," Penelope exclaimed. "So many are important business associates of daddy's.

"It's so nice to get away from the wedding craziness for a while. I love everything my mother has organized but now that we're getting closer to the actual day it's getting a little overwhelming."

"I'll say," Kyle agreed and his bride glared at him.

"Could I speak with you downstairs," she said between clenched teeth.

"You mean below. Boats don't have a downstairs. It's below."

"There are stairs involved, aren't there?" Penelope asked sweetly and Kyle realized he was in serious trouble.

"Er, yes, dear. We can talk below." His bride glared at him. "Downstairs," he amended.

The newlyweds disappeared below as Cassandra placed a covered tray onto a small table. "Some fruit and cheese as snacks. Later we'll grill some steaks and chicken. I hope no one's in a hurry to get back to the hotel. The captain said today promises to be a really good sail and we can stay out all day if we like."

"It's marvelous," Laura said. "I'm sorry that little Petey is too young to come sailing, but I wasn't sure what kind of a sailor he'd make. The hotel has such an excellent baby-sitting service that I only feel a little guilty leaving him behind." She tucked some of her flyaway hair into a ponytail. "I haven't been sailing in years. Did you have your yacht built by Yarmouth Boats?" she asked Peter.

He grinned. "Yes. Not many people recognize Sanders's work."

"He's the best. One of my stepfathers ordered two boats from Yarmouth and he spent many winter hours poring over their catalogue. He was always buying new accessories."

Peter leaned back against the yacht's railing and looked out over Lake Michigan. "I was surprised by how much I enjoyed sailing. Once I figured out I loved it, I bought the best boat I could find. If you can't enjoy the things you buy there's no point. I don't like to acquire just for the sake of ownership. You have quite an eye."

"We're almost ready to leave," Cassandra said.

"So soon?" Clint asked. He'd liked sitting on a chair as the boat was moored to the dock. That was as far as he wanted to go out into the water.

"Can you untie the aft?"

Clint realized Cassandra was asking him. "Er, sure." He looked to the back of the boat wondering what she was talking about.

Laura caught his eyes and nodded toward the front of the boat. "Let me do it," she said. "I'm afraid my husband isn't much of a sailor. He's much more comfortable riding a horse across his property rather than towing in lines or tying sailor's knots." She took a few steps forward. "Why don't you entertain Cassandra while I help Peter take us out."

With quick easy steps she made her way "aft" and began to do something with the ropes. Clint knew she was untying them from their mooring but as he wished they could sit by the lulling waters of the dock all day, he didn't do much more than appreciate the elegance of her movements. "If I didn't know better I'd say you two were still honeymooners," Cassandra said.

"We feel like honeymooners," Clint answered automatically, concentrating on his stomach. It remained quietly in place. "Do you love sailing as much as Laura does?"

"I love it especially when I take over the helm. It looks

like we're almost ready—dammit, that's Tom Watson with a briefcase." A blond-haired man with glasses was running down the pier toward the *Boston Belle* waving his arms. "Peter promised me he wouldn't work today."

Cassandra stalked to the gangplank where her husband met the panting Tom Watson.

"I didn't think I'd make it in time. I have the papers for the Campbell deal. You need to review them."

As Watson held out the attaché case to his boss, Cassandra touched her husband's arm. "You promised you wouldn't work on anything during the wedding. These days are supposed to be about us."

Tom Watson looked worriedly from angry wife to his boss. "We're under a very tight deadline with these negotiations. The lawyers are concerned about some of the points, we need your decision by tomorrow morning."

Peter slipped his arm around his wife's waist. "I promised my wife. Leave the documents at the hotel. I'll review them this evening. Tell my secretary to make arrangements to have them picked up tomorrow morning at 7:00 a.m."

Tom's face paled as his boss didn't take the outstretched briefcase. "Peter, er, I think you should look at the documents today. I can stay ashore and pick them up when you come back in on the boat."

"No, I'm on vacation. Leave the briefcase at the hotel."

"The documents are very important. You called this deal your baby," Tom insisted.

Peter reached for the case but Cassandra moved a little bit faster. "Fine, you can work on the documents later, first we're sailing."

"Dear, if I can review the documents immediately, we'll have more time to enjoy ourselves."

"No," Cassandra said very firmly. "I know you, once

you start working you lose all track of time. We have guests," she pointed toward Laura and Clint and the young lovers who had reappeared on deck, "first we'll sail and have lunch and then if you insist you can work on your very important deal." She leaned and kissed her husband on his cheek and whispered something in his ear.

Peter smiled at his wife. "Send a courier to the hotel tomorrow morning. And Tom, thanks for getting them to me."

Tom Watson nodded in relief. "I apologize Mrs. Monroe for disrupting your holidays." He turned around and left.

Holding the briefcase Cassandra went below deck, appearing a few minutes later without the case. Peter, Cassandra and Laura finished untying the boat, unfurling sails and following the captain's orders until the boat was past the harbor and sailing at a brisk pace on the lake.

Laura sat next to Clint who was concentrating on his stomach. "We need to find out what's inside that briefcase," she said.

Clint breathed in and out. "Peter became much more responsive after Watson insisted how important the documents were."

"Called it Peter's baby." Laura waved at Peter who was securing a mast. Penelope and Kyle found themselves a cozy seat at the front of the boat, away from the others, and snuggled into it. "I think that's the last we'll see of the bride and groom for the rest of this trip."

"Young love." Clint shrugged and then wished he hadn't when his stomach lurched.

"Hmmph. It's easy to confuse lust with love."

"Not for me. Do you do that?"

"My love life is none of your business, cowboy. We need some kind of distraction so one of us can get that

briefcase." She looked through her tote bag. "Excellent."
She pulled out a small camera.

"What is that, your spy camera?"

A smile twitched on Laura's lips. "Okay, I had a few too
many fantasies about being one of *Charlie's Angels* in my
childhood, but I do like to be prepared when I'm out on a
case. Here they come."

Clint carefully raised his head to see Cassandra carrying a plate of food past her husband and kiss him. Peter
looped his arm around her waist and they walked toward
Clint and Laura.

"I could fall overboard and while they rescue me you
could go below and open the briefcase and photograph its
contents," Laura joked.

"I'd have to jump in to rescue you since I'm a heroic
cowboy so madly in love with you."

"Cowboys don't do water rescues."

"This one does." He decided to concentrate on Laura's
pretty ankles but the boat kept moving, lurching back and
forth.

"I guess the same problem exists if you fall overboard."

"Right. Plus I can't swim. I don't want to drown."

"What do you mean you can't swim?"

He shrugged. "Two Horse Junction isn't famed for its
beachfront." Thank goodness. If he got off this boat he
was never stepping foot on another one as long as he
lived.

"I don't want you to drown either."

"Thank you."

"I don't want to have to explain Amber's baby to Captain Clark. What else can we do?"

"I could be violently seasick giving you time to get to
the briefcase and play *Charlie's Angels*." Clint got out each
word slowly and deliberately, focusing on breathing

through his nose. It didn't help. The boat pitched backwards and forwards and backwards and forwards and he clamped his head between his knees.

"You're really good," Laura said admiringly. She leaned down next to him and wiped sweat off his forehead with some tissues from her tote bag. "Darling," she cooed, "are you feeling ill?" She turned to the Monroe's, "I think my husband is taking a minute to get his sea legs."

"He looks awful," Cassandra said.

Indeed Clint did. His face had turned white under his tan and he was starting to shake. Laura took one of the bottles of water from the cooler, and passed it to him. "You really are sick," she whispered accusingly.

"Use it as a distraction," he muttered.

"We should wet some towels," Laura suggested, hoping she could get them—and the briefcase. She felt guilty at abandoning Clint, but this was their chance.

"I'll tell the captain to turn around and head back to shore," Peter said.

"No," Clint muttered. "I'll be better in a little while if I can just lie down. I don't want to spoil the day." He stood and swayed on his feet. Laura tucked herself under his arm and he leaned heavily against her.

"He was like this on the cruise sometimes as well. If he can lie down for a little while he might be better."

With Clint leaning against her she headed them toward the stairs and with Peter's assistance they managed to get Clint to the bench seat of the small living area below. Clint groaned and covered his face with his arm. Laura grabbed some dish towels, dampened them with water from the kitchen's tap and put the cloth on his forehead.

Peter shook his head as he stared at his incapacitated

guest. "I'm going to tell the captain to take us back to shore. Clint should have said he was a poor sailor."

Laura saw the briefcase on the floor against the counter that separated the galley from the living area. Clint made a retching sound and she grabbed the wastebasket and handed it to Clint who promptly threw up into it.

"Maybe you're right," she told Peter. "I thought he only had a weak stomach on the ocean, I should have known he'd only want to come sailing because I love it so much."

Peter took the stairs two at a time to talk to the captain. Laura grabbed the briefcase and tried to open it. It was locked, but she knew how to flip the flimsy locks with a slim wire, like one of the pins she'd used to hold back her hair. She pulled out a hairpin as Clint groaned and then heaved into the wastepaper basket again.

"Are you alright?" she asked as she fiddled with the lock.

"Just open the damn case. If I hear someone on the stairs before you're finished I'll manage something especially distracting."

"What you won't do for that promotion." Laura flipped open the locks and lifted the lid. Inside were a number of legal-size manilla folders. She skimmed through them, they seemed like legal and financial documents for an acquisition. Several paragraphs were highlighted, the questions written in the margins for Peter to answer. Under the legal folders was a jiffy envelope that had already been opened. She looked inside and found two bundles of thousand dollar bills and another document. There had to be at least fifty thousand dollars.

"We've turned around," Cassandra called out from the top step and Laura took a quick shot of the paper with her camera, shoved the money and document back into the envelope, slammed shut the briefcase and dove forward to put it back where she found it.

By the time Cassandra was on the bottom step, Laura was kneeling next to Clint, mopping his brow, the very image of the devoted wife. "We should be back in port in about half an hour."

"Thank you," Laura said gratefully. She settled herself next to Clint and wiped his face.

"Did you find anything?" he mumbled.

"Yes." She told him about the money and the papers as she kept a cool cloth on his forehead. "Why didn't you tell me you were such a bad sailor?"

"We needed a day with the Monroes. Plus you found something. So it was worth it." He leaned over and retched into the bucket.

Laura realized as she cleaned him up that she would have done the same thing. Feeling incredibly domestic she began to tell him about her childhood at a boarding school in Switzerland to distract him. His lips twitched when she described how she and her roommate used to sneak out of their rooms.

She was beginning to realize that she and Clint had a lot more in common than she would have ever imagined. They were both ambitious, determined to be considered on their own merits and they knew next to nothing about babies. What other surprises were in store?

7

HOURS LATER Clint woke in bed and lay perfectly still checking to see if the room was bobbing up and down. To his immense relief he was on solid ground.

Then he remembered and groaned.

He'd been sick twice more before the damned boat had finally stopped moving. Each time after he'd finished vomiting, Laura had cleaned him up and then continued with her silly schoolgirl stories. Once they had finally made it safely back to land, she'd gotten him a clean shirt from Peter and helped him change into the borrowed polo. She'd practically had to carry him off the boat to his car and into the passenger seat. She drove him back to the hotel and put him to bed, where he'd fallen dead asleep.

He looked at his watch and saw that it was after nine o'clock. The whole damn afternoon had been wasted while he'd recovered from his bout of seasickness. He sniffed the air around him and realized a shower was the first order of business before he could look for Laura and ask her if she'd gotten any further with the case, or to thank her again.

He recalled that he'd mumbled apologies to her in the car while she'd told him to stop worrying and that her Florence Nightingale act had impressed Peter Monroe even further. It couldn't have worked out any better than if they'd planned it, but Clint knew better. Laura had been so damn sweet and helpful and all he'd ever done was judge her and have lustful thoughts about her. He was not behaving like the gentleman his mama had raised. As soon as he saw Laura he was going to apologize to her.

But first the shower.

He was halfway to the bathroom when he heard little Petey cry. Laura must have the child in the sitting room. Thank goodness for Petey and Laura because they were the only effective part of their undercover team. He decided he should apologize first and opened the door to the living room.

Vince Garrow was pacing the room holding Petey against his shoulder trying to soothe the fussing baby. He looked up at the sound of the door opening, his pallid face even paler with worry. "Good, you're awake. I think this baby is either teething or auditioning for a remake of *The Exorcist*. I'm a federal agent trained in forensic accounting and have more than a passing knowledge of criminal psychology. I am *not* a highly paid baby-sitter."

Holding the baby out to Clint, Garrow stopped dead in his tracks. "What is that rank odor?" He sniffed the air and then sniffed Petey's diaper. Then he leaned in to Clint and sniffed again. "It's you!" he said, recoiling away from Clint.

Clint stepped backward. "Our day at the sea didn't agree with me. I'm sure Laura told you all about it." Laura and Garrow had probably shared a good laugh over his weak stomach.

Garrow sniffed the air again and shook his head. "Whew, that's ripe. Laura never mentioned it. She said you were asleep and asked me to look after the baby until you woke up. I thought you'd gotten too much sun or had one too many cups of rum punch."

"A hangover would be better than how I feel right

now." His legs still felt like overcooked noodles as he went to the minifridge and took out a bottle of water.

Clint unscrewed the bottle cap and gulped half of the liquid contents before nodding. "Didn't make much of an impression with the Monroes, I'm afraid."

Garrow smiled. "On the contrary. Laura said that Peter thought even more of you for doing something she loved and you didn't care much for."

"Is that how she worded it? *Didn't much care for.*"

"Yes."

"Where did Laura go?" he asked.

"She decided to check out the Monroe's suite. They're dining with the bride's parents tonight. The two of you were invited to dinner as well, but Laura declined since you were indisposed." His mouth twitched. "Now I know why no one asked anything about why you weren't feeling well. Laura thought this was the ideal time to search the Monroes' rooms."

"She's by herself? Why didn't you go with her? Or better yet, why aren't *you* doing the illegal breaking and entering? What if Laura gets caught?" Clint's stomach clenched and he worried he was about to be hit by another bout of seasickness.

Garrow didn't look worried. "She can talk herself out of the situation, she's a bright girl. If Peter Monroe found me in his hotel room he'd recognize me as a former employee and become suspicious. The one advantage we have going for us at this wedding is the fact that Peter Monroe is relaxed and off his guard. If he and Nicholas are planning to meet they may be less cautious than they would be in other circumstances. A wedding makes everyone act differently. It's our best advantage."

"You mean our *only* advantage."

"No," Garrow smiled. "You and Carter make a good

team. I'm beginning to think that we might actually have a chance of cracking this case. She told me about the money in the briefcase. I sent the film to be developed although Laura's afraid she was too rushed to take a legible picture. I've got a Russian translator on standby just in case. Now go and shower before Petey becomes nauseous and decides to contribute his own baby puke."

Clint did as he was told, stripping off his clothes and bundling them up into a plastic garbage bag. He was going to throw them down the incinerator the first chance he got—after he finished yelling at Laura for going to search the Monroes' rooms by herself.

Not that she'd be in any real danger, he reassured himself as he stepped under the hot water. This was the way he liked his water, hot and out of a tap, not rolling around in a great big open expanse...he put his arm against the wall for support and waited for the nausea to pass. Think about Laura instead, he decided.

Garrow thought he and Laura made a good team. Clint was beginning to think so as well. Now that he'd had a moment to think about it, he wasn't really surprised that Laura hadn't told Garrow about Clint's humiliation. He recalled how he had leaned on her as they'd walked along the dock to his sports car. She'd driven back to the hotel without saying much to him and then she'd had the car valet-parked so she could help him to their room. She'd directed him to the big honeymoon bed, pulled off his shoes, wiped his forehead, tucked the covers up to his chin and left him to recover in peace. She'd checked on him a couple of times and refilled his water glass.

He finished showering, toweled off and put on a pair of jeans and a white T-shirt, anxious to go after Laura. Garrow was waiting for him in the living room. "I put the baby to sleep in the crib," he pointed to the portable crib they were using. Garrow put on his jacket. "I'll take the service elevator just in case the Monroes finish dinner early."

"Wait, I want to go after Laura."

Garrow shrugged. "Sorry, but I'm not baby-sitting any longer. Your partner will be fine. I have some paperwork I need to fill out at the office before I take up my baby-sitting duties again. Tomorrow's the big day."

Clint frowned.

"The wedding. Kyle Chandler and Penelope York will tie the knot in front of five hundred of their parents' closest friends. Glad I don't have to put up with any of that nonsense."

"You're not married?"

"No way. Can't put in the hours at SFI you need to get ahead *and* have a wife and family."

Clint felt the same way. That's why he was putting in his time now. Soon he'd be able to go home to Texas and fall in love with the right kind of girl, get married and start a family. He thought three kids would be good, although if his wife was willing to go for more he'd be more than happy to do his husbandly duties. More than happy. He looked forward to a very good married sex life.

He'd always preferred the sex that came about as part of a relationship. One-night stands did nothing more than scratch an itch—and the empty feeling that something was missing from his life was back again the next day.

The idea of being with one woman until "death do us part," sleeping in the same bed every night, sharing a life was what excited him. Wouldn't Ms. Laura Carter be shocked to learn that about him: he was an old-fashioned boy at heart.

He thought about his mother's top three candidates to be Mrs. Clint Marshall. He wondered if they felt the same way he did about marriage. He knew that Laura didn't even believe in the institution of marriage, much less the idea of being married to *him*, much less being married in a place like Two Horse Junction. Now why was he thinking about her? With Garrow gone Clint had nothing to do until Laura came back. Was this what Cassandra felt like when Peter was working on a deal?

He checked on little Petey but the child was asleep with one fist curled next to his mouth, his breathing even. He leaned down and breathed deeply—a scent of talcum powder and baby. He felt a rush of affection for the infant. Petey brought the picture of his future into focus with sharp clarity. The future Mrs. Marshall holding a child with blue eyes and wheat-blond hair. Ignoring the fact that his imaginary child looked very much like Laura, he touched Petey's forehead. "Don't worry, little guy. I'll take care of you until your mother comes back. No one is going to take you away from her."

LAURA HAD BEEN unable to sit in the hotel room and wait for Clint to recover, so she'd decided to follow Peter Monroe. In her experience, once the suspects began to move, the activity increased dramatically. While she'd never actually used her little camera on a case before and was unsure of the quality of the photos, Garrow had sent her film from the boat to be developed. More important, she'd recognized Cyrillic, the Russian alphabet, as the text on the document. Having found the money and the paperwork made it look like Monroe really was guilty.

Laura was surprised to feel disappointment. She'd liked Peter because of how fond he was of little Petey. But then she remembered a case of hers in Boston involving an up-and-coming drug dealer who had been a great parent. They'd managed to put him away for twenty years. His kids would be married with children of their own before he got out again, she thought suddenly.

Garrow had been so thrilled to hear what she and Clint had uncovered that he had wanted to be the one following Monroe, but she reminded him that Monroe would recognize Garrow if he caught him, but not Laura. There were wedding guests milling throughout the hotel. Her instincts were telling her that Monroe was finding the wedding a perfect public place to meet with Vasili.

First she'd stopped by Peter and Cassandra's suite ostensibly to thank them for a lovely day and to report that her husband was feeling much better. Dressed in a blue cocktail dress, Cassandra had answered the door and said she was on her way to the bride's parents' suite for drinks and she'd swept Laura along with her. As she sipped a sparkling water, she wondered when Peter would show. Just as she put down her drink thinking she would wander through more of the hotel, she spied Nicholas Vasili flirting with Cassandra.

Keeping her eyes on them she circled the room, getting closer and looking for Peter at the same time. Instead, when she stepped out onto the balcony she found Tom Watson, Peter's VP of legal affairs staring at Cassandra and Vasili. "Were you invited to the wedding as well?" Laura asked.

Watson jumped at the sound of her voice. "No, Monroe called me to say he'd have the documents I gave him on the boat ready. Cassie suggested I come to the party to kill some time."

Laura wondered when *Cassie* had had the opportunity to talk to Watson. "Do you have to spend a lot of your free time chasing after Peter?"

Watson shrugged. "It comes with the job." His eyes kept straying toward the windows.

"I suppose there are perks. Have you ever escorted Mrs. Monroe in Peter's stead?"

Watson turned his full attention to her. "Where's your husband?"

"He's recovering from the boat ride, but you're right, I should check on him."

She and Watson stepped back into the party together. Laura wanted to go check on little Petey and Clint so she headed to the elevators, but when she saw the cars stopping on every single floor she decided to walk down the ten flights instead. Just as she was opening the door to the stairwell she heard male voices and looked back. Vasili and Peter Monroe were stepping into the same elevator. She raced back to the cars but the doors had already closed. With frustration she watched it head up to the penthouse suites. She ran up the stairs but by the time she made it to the top floor there was no one in the hallway. "Damn and damn." She decided to get Garrow.

She took the stairs back down to her floor and walked in to her suite just in time to hear Clint crooning to Petey. Her heart did a bizarre flip.

"That's very sweet," Laura said behind him.

A little embarrassed, he turned to see her next to the door. "I didn't hear you come in."

"I think you were singing to Petey."

He felt heat stain his cheeks. "My mother always sang to my brothers."

"And you probably did the same when your mother wasn't home. I always wished I could have had a brother or sister."

He smoothed the tuft of hair on Petey's head and turned to Laura. She was dressed in slim-fitting black silk pants and a sleeveless black knit top that clung to every inch of her. He felt such a zing of sexual awareness that he froze, calming his body back to normal. He told himself he didn't want to make love to Laura Carter because he could not imagine her participating with passion. Then again, it would be quite a challenge to make her want him.

"Why are you looking at me like that?" Laura asked.

"I'm trying to decide whether to throttle you or simply yell at you."

She raised her chin. "I'm waiting."

"Don't ever go out to play investigation without back up."

"You were indisposed and I needed Garrow to look after the baby. I didn't want to miss this chance."

He moved in closer. "Not good enough."

Laura put her hands on her hips and stepped toward him. "I made a decision and I'll stick by it. Let me remind you that I supported you when you decided to keep baby Petey for his mother." She poked her finger into his chest. "So don't tell me what I can or cannot do."

He caught her hand when she would have pushed him harder and felt another jolt. "Damn," he said under his breath but she heard him.

"I will not have you swearing at me, either."

"Did you find anything in the Monroes' rooms?"

"I went to a cocktail party with Cassandra. Tom Watson was there as well mooning over her. Vasili was there, too."

"He's not expected until tomorrow."

"There's more. I saw Vasili and Peter Monroe leave the party together. I think they went back to Peter's rooms, but I couldn't confirm it. We should phone Garrow. Let go of my hand."

He dropped her hand, unaware he'd still been grasping it.

"You must be feeling better if you want to fight with me." She brushed a loose strand of blond hair off her face.

He ached to run his fingers through her long soft hair. He mentally shook himself; there was no way he was going to tell her what he'd really like to do with her. "Much better, thank you." He stepped away from her. "I should apologize, that is, my behavior earlier—"

"Yes, you were very rude. Apology accepted."

She used her royal tone but he realized she was putting on the princess routine because of the sizzle of electricity running between them. Deliberately he took a step forward, she took one back. "Not now, I meant on the boat."

She waved her hand. "Oh, that. Don't worry about it. Except you should have told me you got seasick."

"I told you I didn't like boats."

"I thought you meant you didn't like boats, not that you got violently ill at the sight of a wave."

"It took more than a sight."

She seemed to be relieved that they were on neutral ground. "Do you feel better?"

"Much. Thanks for mopping my brow."

"Peter Monroe found me a very loving and dutiful wife. It could not have been better if we'd planned it." She loosened her hair out of its sleek ponytail. He watched dry mouthed as it fell around her shoulders, a strand brushing against her cheek. He clenched his fists as his side. He didn't want to like anything about Laura Carter. She was annoying. She wasn't the kind of woman he wanted to be with.

"Is that the kind of husband you want? Someone you'll end up taking care of? Someone to boss around?"

"The last thing in the world I plan to do is get married."

"Why?"

She looked away from him. "The women in my family

have a bad track record with marriage. I was engaged once, and that's as close as I ever want to get to walking down the aisle."

"I never thought I would find something that scares you."

Laura shrugged her shoulders. "I'm not scared. I'm a realist."

Clint didn't like how sad she looked. "Marriage is the ultimate union between a man and a woman."

"Half of the marriages end in divorce," she shot back.

"That's either because they picked the wrong person or they didn't try hard enough," he countered.

"If you're such a fan of the institution, why haven't you shackled yourself with the proverbial ball and chain?"

"I'm being smart about my choice," he answered in calm tones. "I'm going to marry a girl from Two Horse Junction."

"Do you have someone waiting for you back home?" Laura's voice was soft as she looked at him with a curious expression.

"No, that wouldn't have been right. But I know the single women back home and fully expect to fall in love with someone appropriate."

"You expect to fall in love with someone appropriate," she mimicked, her previous expression replaced by the anger sparking her eyes. Now why was she mad at him?

"I suppose you have all her qualities picked out." Laura continued. "Why, your mother probably keeps you abreast of all the single women in town. You'd better let her know that she needs to add a strong stomach to her list of requirements."

"There's not much sailing back home, but yes I know what I'm looking for."

"A woman with child-bearing hips I shouldn't wonder." She ran her hands over her own hips. "Luckily I don't qualify."

His eyes followed the path her hands had taken and he remembered what she had felt like in his arms when they had kissed on the dance floor. "No, but there are some women a man doesn't want to marry."

She gasped. "So you think I'm worth sleeping with, but not marrying!"

"You're the one who said she doesn't want to get married. I want to get married. I want a woman who wants the same things I do."

"To live in a small town and have a house full of kids."

"Yes."

When had Clint moved so close to her? She stuck out her chin. "But you'd like to sleep with me. I've gotten under your skin and you'd like to find out why. Find out what I'd be like in bed."

His hands shot out and grabbed her upper arms, lifting her slightly. "Don't try to pretend. You're the one who wants me. You're dying to know if the cowboy has some tricks you've never experienced." His lips were only a breath away from hers. "You want me."

She didn't try to break his grip, instead her blue eyes glittered as she smiled and ran her tongue across her bottom lip. "Don't be ridiculous. You want me."

"Liar," he taunted, as his fingers caressed her arms. She sighed and her gaze fell on his lips and he felt a deep pulsing need to kiss her, to devour her mouth, to crush her against his body and make love to her. Still not sure if he was going to do this, if sanity would return any second, he moved his hands up her shoulders, along the soft skin of her neck to cup her head.

"All you can think about is kissing me, getting me naked and on that big bed," she said huskily, her eyes shooting waves of blue flame at him. Her uneven breathing was matched by his.

His lips brushed against hers. "You're the one who wants me, admit it." He smiled at her as he traced a circle on her earlobe.

She smiled back and ran her tongue along his bottom lip. She was rewarded when Clint shuddered. Leaning forward slightly she pressed her lips fully against his and kissed him like she'd been thinking about all day. She smelled leather and the masculine scent that was Clint's when his arms wrapped tight around her and he crushed her against his body.

Laura loved the feel of his hard body against hers and fire scorched her flesh where he explored her body. He ran his hands up over her hips to her breasts, teasing her nipple erect. Desire pulsed through her veins making her want more and more as she angled her mouth against his, her tongue mating with his.

Finally Clint broke the kiss. "Damn." He stepped away from her and stared at the big honeymoon bed. "I must be plum crazy." He began to pull off one of his boots.

Laura heard the blood pounding in her head as she stared at the bed. She could stop this right now if she wanted, if she was smart. She didn't want to be smart. "Don't start that Texan talk with me, cowboy." Laura wrapped her arms around herself as if she were suddenly cold, and she was without Clint's arms around her. "What are you doing?"

"I'm taking off my boots." He sat down on the bed and pulled off the second boot. He dropped it on the floor. The loud plunk reverberated through the silence of the room. "Take off your clothes," he said, his voice hoarse, his eyes glittering as he raked her body.

"What?" Laura gulped nervously, wishing Clint would

just grab her and pull her onto the bed. Why did this man always have to be so ornery and insist she admit she wanted him?

Clint undid the buttons on his shirt, and left it hanging open against his bare chest as his molten steel eyes met her shocked gaze. She felt the heat from his gaze as their eyes locked. *Oh good*, was her only thought, *he wanted her*.

"Strip," he repeated. "I want to see you naked."

Not giving herself a chance to think and stop her irrational behavior, she took hold of the bottom of her black sweater and pulled it over her head. She dropped the garment on the floor, and with a female instinct she didn't know she was capable of, she bent over to shake out her hair and threw back her head. She was rewarded by the sharp intake of Clint's breath. She was glad she'd chosen to wear a sheer black bra trimmed with lace. Clint was staring at her breasts and her nipples hardened in reaction to the raw need on his face.

"You're beautiful," he whispered. "I want to see all of you."

Suddenly Laura felt happy. She kicked off her black sneakers and socks. She felt sexy and gorgeous and wanted and she was going to make love with Clint. Her every fantasy was going to come true, and it was already starting off better than she'd ever fantasized.

The cowboy and the princess. Yahoo!

"More," Clint said. "You're still not naked."

She flashed him a wicked grin and turned around. She undid the button on her jeans and then unzipped her pants, the sound unnaturally loud in the room. Continuing to play to an unknown sensual part of her, she wiggled her backside as she began to slowly lower her pants. With the talent of a born coquette, she inched her jeans past her hips, looking over her shoulder at Clint. He had a slightly glazed expression on his face. "Keep going," he said.

Slowly she finished wiggling her way out of her jeans and turned around to face him wearing her matching sheer black panties and bra. She grinned. "Your turn."

"First your bra. Take off your bra."

"If I take off my bra," she lowered one strap, "you'll take off your clothes."

"Faster than a Texas lightning storm," he drawled, but his eyes belied the amusement in his voice. Desire and impatience showed in his eyes sending heat through her.

"No, slow," she got out from between dry lips. "I want you to strip real nice and slow. I want to watch."

He nodded. Feeling more sexual than she ever had in her life she reached behind her back to unhook the bra. With her arms clasped across her breasts she let the wisp of lace fall to the floor. Clint shot off the bed and he was in front of her. "I want to touch you," he said. "Please."

She let her arms drop to her sides and watched his gaze lower to her breasts. "Fantastic," he rasped. He reached out with one hand and cupped her breast, running a thumb over her nipple. He cupped her other breast and she moaned as he caressed her sensitive flesh. "I can't wait to taste you, to scrape those rosy nipples with my teeth and make you cry out with pleasure." He began to lower his head to her breasts and she wanted his mouth on her, warm and hungry, but first—

She pushed him back. "Your turn. Strip for me, cowboy." She sauntered to the bed and leaned back with her arms supporting her weight behind her.

"Do you know what you look like?"

"What?"

"Like a lady of the house who is about to be pleasured by her stable boy."

"You're my cowboy, not a stable boy. Now pleasure me and strip."

Clint laughed and began to take off his shirt. He turned around and revealed one bare shoulder then the other. He turned back to face her and flashed his chest. Then he dropped the shirt on the floor and Laura's mouth went dry as his gaze captured hers. Suddenly there wasn't any more time for play, she wanted him on her, in her immediately. He held her gaze as he walked toward her. She heard the zipper on his jeans but she was held captive by his eyes.

Then he was on her, his body hot all over hers and she felt his erection pressing through his jeans at her and realized that he hadn't stopped to take off his pants. His mouth was on hers and he was kissing her furiously as if he couldn't get enough. She met him kiss for kiss as they rolled around on the honeymoon bed. They hit the bedpost at the bottom of the bed and she lay on top of him. He tore his mouth away from hers, his lips continuing to brush kisses along her jawline over to her ear. "You feel so good." His hands stroked down her back in long strokes and then along her buttocks. Finally he cupped her behind in his hands, caressing her.

"I, oh..." she kissed his chest and then licked a drop of salty sweat from him.

"You're killing me," he said, his hands moving her against him so that her moist center was grinding against his jean-clad erection.

She heard them groan together, then she pushed herself up on her elbows on his chest. Clint continued to push her lower body against him and she felt too close to a climax. "Clint, I'm ready now, please." He stopped his erotic pumping and smiled. "Baby, you're going to be a lot more ready before we go for it."

"I'm serious, Clint. Take off your jeans and I'll prove it to you. By the time I'm finished with you, you won't be able to imagine what you ever saw in the girls back at Four Pony Stop."

"That's awful big talk for a Boston blue blood. Us Texans know how to get hot and sweaty."

Laura grinned back at him and realized she was having a good time. She couldn't remember a time when she was able to tease and laugh with the man she was in bed with.

She reached for his jeans and began to lower them down his lean hips. "C'mon, cowboy. I want you naked. I want to see if Texas really does make everything bigger."

Clint pulled her to him and kissed her on the mouth, the force of his desire making her collapse against his chest. She had to wrap her arms tight around his shoulders to hold herself upright.

Then she was falling back and realized she was lying on her back on the honeymoon bed. Clint was nudging her legs apart with a naked thigh. At some point during their delirious kiss he'd stripped so that he was as naked as she was. His hand ran along her inner thigh and stroked her readiness.

"Clint," she said on a gasp as he stroked her sensitive flesh, "please, I—"

"It's all right, Princess. You don't need to beg. We're going to go together."

She moved against him. "Not that. I want to see you." She ran her hand down his chest and over his stomach.

"I can't stop," he said between gritted teeth as she felt his penis brush against her entrance.

"Please," she said.

His storm-gray eyes locked with hers and she had to wet her lips at the passion she saw burning inside.

"I can't stop. I have to be inside you. Here," he took her

hand and lowered it to his erection. "Careful, I'm so hot for you..." She circled her fingers around the width of him and let out a breath as she explored the length of him.

"Oh my, big is an understatement."

"Glad I meet your approval." He grabbed her hand away and raised both her hands over her head. She felt him seeking entrance and raised her legs, locking them around his hips. She wondered if she could take all of him, but then he was inside her and she gasped.

"All right?" he asked, holding himself still inside her.

She nodded as her body adjusted to him. "You're a little more man than us Boston blue bloods are used to."

He withdrew, then filled her again and her blood sang. "Just perfect," she said and laughed out loud.

Clint joined her laughter for a few seconds but then he began to love her. He let go of her hand as he lowered his mouth to her lips and his hands loved her body. She stopped laughing as the sensation and emotions filled her, just as Clint was filling her. This was the most serious thing she had ever done.

She called out his name when she climaxed and heard him shout out at the same time.

He collapsed on top of her and rolled them to the side holding her close against him as they came back to earth. Slowly she regained her breath and her composure, but she felt like Clint still owned a part of her.

Ridiculous. All she had done was finally scratch her itch.

She traced a finger along his sweat-dampened chest.

"Damn, but that was fine," he said.

"Very agreeable," she said.

"Agreeable," he snorted. "You sure are an ornery woman."

She raised herself on one elbow and as the strands of

her hair brushed along his chest, Clint sucked in a big mouthful of air.

She smiled with satisfaction. "Mother always taught me to give praise where it was due, but not to go overboard."

He rolled over onto his back as she sat astride him. He was still inside her and she felt him growing hard. He rolled his hips and she gasped. "I'll show you agreeable."

She closed her eyes so she could concentrate on the delicious sensations. "This is very...agreeable." She'd meant to sound regal but her voice came out husky and rather breathless. She opened her eyes and grinned at him. "Ride 'em cowboy."

8

LAURA WOKE suddenly feeling that something was very different, and opened her eyes to the ceiling of an unfamiliar room. She looked to her right and saw a bedstand and alarm clock. Then she remembered she was on an undercover assignment—the idiot Monroe case—with Clint Marshall. So why did she feel so—

She bolted upright. She had slept with Clint Marshall! She moaned and flopped backward on the bed. How could she have been so stupid? Why hadn't she controlled her weakness; her ridiculous passion for the overgrown cowboy.

"Mmmph," said something behind her.

She gasped as Clint's arm snaked out from under the covers and wrapped around her waist, pulling her on top of him.

"What do you think you're doing?" she asked as she tried to raise her head off his chest. She resisted the impulse to run her fingers over his chest or place her lips on his masculine nipple.

"Snuggling," he said in a sleep-roughened voice. He traced a circle along the small of her back with light, tantalizing fingers.

"Stop it."

He kissed the top of her shoulder, sending a wave of heat through her body. "Stop it," she repeated weakly.

"Okay." He moved his lips to her shoulder and sank his

teeth into her skin very gently, sending a jolt straight down to her toes. He cupped her breast with a palm, running his thumb over her taut nipple. "We've got time..."

"No."

"That's not what you said last night. Let me change your mind again." With his hand behind her head he pulled her down for his kiss, his lips firm and inviting, coaxing her back to that passion that flared so quickly between them.

She pulled herself away, pushing herself up on her arms so that they were nose to nose. At the very least, she could face her mistake. "No. We have work to do."

His gray eyes studied hers. "Having regrets already? I never thought you were a coward."

She pushed herself off him and sat up, pulling one of the dislodged sheets around her. "I am not a coward. I'm not afraid to admit when I've made a mistake." She managed to pull the sheet from Clint and threw the last of it around one shoulder, wrapping herself as tightly as she could.

"Making love with me was a mistake?"

"We didn't make love. It was sex—pure and simple. Sex. That's all."

"Sex." His voice was as cold as his steely eyes. "No matter how tight you wrap yourself up in that sheet you won't be able to erase what we did. I know what you look like naked. I'm not about to forget it anytime soon."

She raised her chin. "I don't forget my mistakes. I remember them so I won't repeat them." Making love with Clint had been her biggest mistake ever. It had also been the best sex ever. Why did this cowboy have to turn out to be the real-life fulfillment of every fantasy she had ever spun about men and lovemaking? If she wasn't careful she'd resume her usual pattern of falling in love with him and changing her life to suit his. Why she'd even end up following him to Two Horse Junction!

She turned her back to him intent on getting to the bathroom. As a result she didn't see him move, and almost tripped when her sheet got caught on something. She tugged but it didn't budge. She turned around and saw that Clint was stepping on the tail of her bedsheet. "Please let me go," she said in her most imperial tone, the one her mother used on the new servants.

Clint stared at her—his eyes hard chips of ice. "As my lady commands." He took his foot off the bedclothes.

Relieved by his unexpected reasonableness she took a deep breath and leaned down slightly when she felt the world tip and twirl around her. Clint had pulled the sheet—and her—to him. She landed hard against his chest and dropping what little she still clutched of the sheet and pushed with her arms hard against his chest. She found herself standing a foot away from him, as naked as he was.

"How dare you?" she demanded.

"I won't be insulted by you. A mistake. You *wanted* me in your bed, or did you forget how you begged me to take you last night?"

Her cheeks flaming in memory of those very words, she moved slightly closer to him to show that he didn't intimidate her in the slightest. "What I remember very clearly is that I gave in to this foolish sexual attraction I had for you. But now that we've..." Words failed briefly as he stared at her in astonishment. "Now that I've tried what you have to offer, my curiosity is sated."

She raised her chin and met his gaze with her ice-queen look. She saw anger, frustration and something else cross his face. She turned slightly to move away when his hands shot out and caught her by the elbows.

"Not so fast, Princess, you were the one who wanted me, remember..."

But she had caught on to him. He was trying to make her angry so that she'd admit what she was really feeling. "That was last night," she said coolly. "As I said, an experiment. For some reason I found your cowboy charm...appealing."

He let go of her arms and took a step back, his gaze slowly travelled down her face and neck, lingered on her breasts, down her body, stopping again on the vee between her legs. She refused to flinch or cover herself.

"Enjoy the view while you can. It will be the last time."

He smiled confidently. "No, it won't."

The gall of the man—thinking all he had to do was drawl a few sweet words and she would want him again. She would never let him know how weak she was. "No."

His smile changed, became warm and seductive and she felt her insides become warm and welcome. "Princess," he stretched the word into an endearment. "When I want you again you'll come running."

She had had her one taste of forbidden fruit and it would last her. Her mother was the one who kept eating until the tree was bare. Laura, however, knew to stop. But like Eve, was one taste already too much?

Laura felt herself weaken. It would be so easy to fall into bed with him. It would be fantastic.

But then she would fall into her familiar pattern: falling for a man who was completely wrong for her. Fitting her life around his until the day he grew tired of her and left. And then she wouldn't even have her old life.

Her mother had had five husbands, not one of whom had hung around longer than a couple of years.

When she'd gotten engaged to Brian, she'd transferred schools to be close to him. Had spent all her time fixing up their apartment, planning their lives, until she'd walked in on him in bed with another woman.

And then there'd been Joe. He'd been a regular guy, a cop in fact. She'd realized she was falling into the same pattern as with Brian, and gotten out. However, she had learned that being a police officer was what she wanted. That's when she'd given up on men and concentrated on becoming a great cop.

She stiffened her spine, raised her chin and glared at him. He looked down at her amused. "Anytime," he said and covered her lips with his.

It was an angry lover's kiss, his mouth crushing hers. She caught the same consuming fire and when he finally released her, they both gasped for breath. His eyes glittered. "Anytime, every time, Princess."

Furious at herself for responding to his caveman tactics, furious at herself for repeating her mistakes, she moved to break away from his possessive embrace when she heard Sweetums whining at her feet, followed by a loud pounding at the door.

"Damn." Clint broke away from her. "Go away," he shouted.

"It's Garrow," the SFI agent called through the bedroom door. Laura realized he'd let himself into their suite and was standing in their living area. She dived for the sheet, wrapped it around herself, grabbed a handful of clothes out of her dresser and flew into the bathroom. She dressed quickly and then splashed cold water on her face staring at her image in the vanity mirror. She looked the same, but she did not feel the same. Last night with Clint had been the most passionate, complete experience of her life. Her few nights with other men paled in comparison. If she was honest, and she usually was, they were nothing in comparison.

How did Clint have such power over her? She'd lusted after him from the moment she'd laid eyes on him, but she'd thought it would fade. She'd thought she could keep her desire a secret—never for a moment had she ever imagined she would end up in Clint's bed. Or he in hers—whichever of them had rights to claim their hotel bed.

She hadn't behaved like herself, either—she'd turned into a wild woman who had been unable to have enough. A woman who had laughed and screamed, and told Clint exactly what she wanted.

Well, fine, she'd itched that scratch. Now she was done. She had to remember that she had a case to solve, a baby to return to his mother, a dog to look after. The faster she solved this insane case the faster she could return to her regular life, and keep herself far away from Clint Marshall.

He was planning to return to Texas soon, anyway. To marry one of those women on his list: Betty Sue, Bobbie Sue or Bootsie Sue. Then he wouldn't be around to devil her any longer. She ignored the sinking feeling in her stomach and straightened her shoulders. Right now she had to face Vince Garrow and his suspicions. Had he let himself into their suite hoping to find the ice princess in bed with the cowboy?

She was aware of her reputation, of what her fellow officers thought. Too many of them believed she was climbing her way to the top flat on her back. She had hoped that if she solved this case, she might gain their respect.

But she'd ruined any chances of that. No one would ever believe that her family played no positive role in her career—quite the reverse, in fact. She sighed and allowed herself to feel sorry for herself for a few seconds.

She had to face Garrow. And Clint.

She stuck her tongue out at herself in the mirror. "Buck

up, ice queen," she said out loud and then frowned. *Buck up?* Now she was talking like Clint.

She walked through the second bedroom where baby Petey was sleeping peacefully to the living room. She stopped dead as Clint grabbed Garrow by the lapels of his worn suit, dragging him to his toes pulling his face within inches of his own. "You are not going to breathe a word of what you think happened to anyone. There is nothing going on between Laura and myself. She doesn't like me. Do I make myself clear?"

"Very clear," Garrow gasped out. "I can't breathe."

Indeed he was turning blue and Clint let him go. Garrow bent over gasping, and then straightened, rubbing his neck. "Hey, listen, if you have a proprietary interest in her, fine. Just telling me she's your woman would have had me backing off."

"She is not my woman," Clint gritted out.

Humiliated, Laura grabbed Sweetums and backed out of the room. There were enough rumors about her before, why had she made the mistake of sleeping with Clint? She made a new entrance talking loudly to Sweetums and this time the men were sitting opposite each other. "Do you have the translations from the documents?"

"I'm expecting them to be sent to me anytime." Garrow patted his laptop. "My friend is going to e-mail me. I pulled some strings with an old girlfriend who translates for the state department." At the word girlfriend Garrow glared at Clint and Laura was afraid they were about to come to blows again.

For some reason she couldn't think of anything to say, and was relieved when a furious knocking at the door interrupted the silence. She motioned for Garrow to hide himself in one of the bedrooms in case it was Monroe and opened it. It was Amber who rushed in. "Quick, close the door, I think Johnny is after me." The young girl looked around the hotel room suspiciously. She considered Garrow and then dismissed him as another cop.

"I thought he was still in jail," Laura said.

Amber shook her head as she put her knapsack on the floor. "Can't trust the legal system. He made bail and he's determined to make me pay. One of the girls told me he was out and looking for me."

"Does he know we have your child?" Clint asked.

"I don't think so." She smiled and her face softened. She wasn't wearing much makeup, and Clint realized once again how young she was. And worried about her baby. As if sensing his mother's presence, Petey began to cry.

"My baby. I want to see him, where is he?"

"He's in the other room, I'll get him." Laura left to get the child.

Garrow raised an eyebrow in Clint's direction, but he didn't say anything. Clint hoped that Garrow realized the child was their secret weapon, and not to question who the child's mother was.

Laura came out cradling Petey in her arms. "Here's the little tyke."

"My baby," Amber cooed as she took the boy into her arms. "Look who's here, it's mommy. Is Petey happy to see his mommy?"

"What did you call him?" Clint asked.

"Petey. I named him Peter."

Laura smiled at Clint and he smiled back. "Peter is a nice name," she said.

Amber stroked her son's head as she rocked him back and forth in her arms. "My grandfather was named Peter. He was really great. I don't know what went wrong with my dad, but if Petey takes after his great-grandfather, he'll turn out okay."

She kissed the top of her son's head. "Can you keep him for another couple of days?"

"Yes," Laura said.

"Who's he?" Amber pointed her head toward Garrow without taking her gaze off Garrow.

"He's a friend of ours. He's been helping us with Petey," Clint answered.

"Are you doing something dangerous? I don't care if you're pulling some kind of scam but I'm trusting you with my son."

"We'd never do anything that would hurt your son," Laura said, putting her arm around Amber. "We're posing as a married couple and having a baby has been a help. Our target likes us as happy parents. That's as far as your son's involvement has gone. We'd never put him in any danger," she repeated.

Garrow apparently decided it was time for him to join in on the conversation. "I'm their supervisor on this assignment, and while the arrival of your baby was a surprise," he looked hard at Clint, "your son has never been in any danger. I promise you it will stay that way."

"What are you going to do about Johnny?" Laura asked Amber. "Can we help? I have a friend at the Social Services office. I could talk to—"

"No, I'm doing this myself. I don't want to talk to the law—that just gets me into trouble, no offense meant."

"But what about your pimp? How are you planning to get away from him?"

Amber smiled. "Don't worry, that I have covered. All I need is a little time for Petey to be somewhere safe away from me."

Clint frowned. "Amber, let me help. If you've cooked up some kind of crazy scheme, it could backfire. Let us—"

"No," Amber's voice was firm. She kissed her son and

handed him back to Laura. "I know what I'm doing," she told Laura, her eyes filled with conviction. "I'm not going to let anything happen to my son."

"Okay," Laura said as she cradled the boy against her. "Your son is beautiful."

Sweetums panted at her feet, looking longingly at her. "Don't worry about the dog, she likes Petey."

Amber laughed. "Maybe you two were meant to look after my son. I'll be back in a day or two." She leaned over to kiss her son again, fiddled with her purse straps. She raised her chin, looked briefly at Clint, "Look after Petey." They remained silent as she left.

"You two astonish me," Garrow said. "Every time I think I've figured out every rule you've broken, you ignore even more." He shook his head.

Laura bristled. "Every rule we've broken has been to help you on your case. Now if you will excuse us, I suggest you find yourself a spare room where you can capture a couple of hours of shut-eye, I have a few things I want to straighten out with my husband." She drawled the words in her best Texas twang.

Garrow considered her. "I could use some sleep. I have the room across the hall from you if you need me for anything."

Laura waited until he exited before she turned on Clint. She picked up Sweetums who picked up on her mood and growled. "How dare you?"

He refused to freeze to the chill in her voice. "A gentleman always protects a woman's honor."

"Is that what you call it? Well, cowboy, I am perfectly capable of looking after myself. I do not need you to help me with my reputation."

"Well you're sure not doing a very good job of it."

Outraged, she wished she had something to throw. "I

am handling the situation the way I see best. I do not need your help."

Clint moved in until they were toe to toe. "You do not always need to do everything by yourself. Sometimes it's fine to accept someone else's help, when it's offered. You take care of Sweetums and Petey. Let me take care of you."

"No," she said. "That's not the way it works for me. I don't want some macho cowboy protecting me. All we had was a one-night stand. That doesn't give you any rights to me."

"I like you, Laura. Let me help you."

"No. Once this case is closed I do not expect to see you again. I do not need your help." Unwilling to look at him another second, unwilling to admit how much her own words hurt her, Laura stalked out the door, slamming it behind her.

9

I TAKE CARE OF MYSELF.

Laura replayed the words in her head as she stood in the hotel corridor. "I *can* take care of myself," she repeated out loud. Suddenly exhausted, she leaned against the wall and took a deep breath to gather her strength.

She needed to be strong, not let this cowboy charmer get to her—especially not to her weaknesses. If she let down her guard, she could let him into her heart and she knew the disastrous consequences that would follow.

While she'd been smart enough not to get married, the two men she'd gotten close to had wanted her to be a different kind of woman. And when she had changed, they still hadn't been satisfied.

No more changing to please others. That was why proving herself on this assignment, on all her assignments, was so crucial to her.

Her family didn't understand her drive, so how could Clint? He came from a family that loved and supported him no matter what his choices. She, on the other hand... She didn't let herself finish her thought about how her family supported her.

The man who was the source of all her troubles opened the door of their hotel suite and stepped out into the hallway with little Petey in a baby carryall and Sweetums in his arms. "You're still here."

"Yes. I was thinking about the case...and what I said to

you. I'm sorry. I was very rude to you and that was inexcusable. You were also right, I was the one who initiated...things between us last night."

"Those *things* are called lovemaking."

She flinched. "Sex. It was just sex," she said very precisely, her face pale.

He felt the anger begin to boil up in him when he looked into her eyes and saw the control she was exerting over herself. He realized that for some reason it was very important that Laura believe what had happened between them was purely physical. He took a step toward her and she stepped back. Laura's eyes followed the movement of his hands as he pet Sweetums and he knew she was remembering how he had touched her last night.

"We had an affair," he said, continuing to pet Sweetums. The dog drooled onto his sleeve but from the way Laura was watching him, it was worth it. Laura was no different than the scared wild horses he had trained on their ranch. He needed to handle her with skill and kindness and they would be back together again in the big bed of the honeymoon suite.

"If that's all you want it to be that's fine with me. I'm not looking to be involved with any snooty Boston heiress."

Laura smiled. "I don't want to get involved with a hick cowboy, either."

He grinned. "Then we're in agreement. Why don't we go get some lunch."

"I'll take Sweetums." She took the dog from Clint's arm, and clipped on its leash. Looking incredibly domestic, Laura with the dog, Clint with the baby in the carryall, they went to the lobby restaurant. Several groups of wedding guests smiled at them as the waitress seated them at a table.

To her surprise Petey didn't fuss, but settled happily in Clint's arms and drooled. She wiped his face with her napkin. "I'm afraid Petey is picking up bad habits from Sweetums. This is very domestic, isn't it?"

Clint grinned. "Very. Makes me look forward to having my own children."

The smile wiped off her face. He reached forward and took her hand. "I'm sorry for being such an idiot last night. And for whatever I just said that made you look so unhappy. I always seem to be saying the wrong thing to you so, here I go again." He paused for a moment as his gray eyes searched her face.

"Did you have an affair with your captain back in Boston?"

Her eyes grew wide as she looked at him. "You're the first person who's actually come out and asked me. No, I didn't."

"Then why did you get transferred to Chicago so quickly? Your family must have pulled strings to get you here."

She tore her piece of bread into smaller and smaller pieces. "My family had everything to do with my transfer to Boston because Uncle Alfred...oh this is much harder to say than I thought. I thought I'd be relieved to tell someone but...Mother didn't like...that is, she thought I'd get over this whim about being a police officer so she asked Uncle Alfred to do something. And well, he's very old-fashioned and he was sure I would be happier being a proper Carter and then, well..."

He reached across the table and took her hand. "What did your uncle do?"

"He started the rumors. I don't think for a second he thought they'd get so out of control, and he never thought about how my captain's poor wife would feel. When the whole thing blew up Uncle Alfred confessed and then he promised to fix things by getting me a job in Chicago."

Clint took both her hands in his and held them.

A stack of papers smacked down on the table between them. "I've got the translations," Garrow announced, appearing suddenly. Clint dropped her hands as Garrow, once again dressed in his bellboy uniform and fake beard, pulled a chair from another table to theirs and sat down, ignoring the intimate scene he'd interrupted. "It's unusual but it's definitely an agreement for an exchange."

"I like the beard. You should think about keeping it." In truth he looked ridiculous, but she hadn't forgiven him for almost walking in on her and Clint.

Laura took the translated documents and read them, frowning. "It sounds like Monroe is buying something for fifty thousand dollars. This doesn't connect to any of the money being laundered through his company."

"I know, but it's enough," Garrow insisted. "My gut says that whatever Monroe is buying will be delivered before this wedding is over. You two are going to stick like glue to the Monroes and catch the delivery. And then you'll arrest him. I don't care if Monroe is buying a painting stolen from the Hermitage or old Cold War secrets, if you can catch them we'll have something. They got Capone for income tax evasion. I'll find something to keep Peter Monroe in jail."

As the waitress dropped off their food, Garrow grabbed half of Laura's sandwich. "What are you two waiting for? You've got a wedding to attend."

THREE HOURS LATER, Laura dabbed her eyes as Kyle Chandler toasted his new bride.

Clint leaned forward. Throughout the church ceremony

and reception he'd been watching Laura and wondering about his attraction to her. She was all wrong for him. To distract himself, he'd then started to reexamine the case against Peter, but found it equally frustrating. All the hard evidence was too circumstantial.

"I thought you didn't believe in weddings and happily ever after," he said.

"Not for myself. But Penelope and Kyle seem to be very much in love. It's sweet. I hope they make it." She drank from her glass of champagne and smiled at him.

He felt it like a blow to his gut; her blue eyes sparkling, her cheeks pink, the champagne glistening off her bottom lip. He leaned forward and brushed his lips across hers tasting the champagne.

"That's what I like to see, a couple still in love after marriage," Peter Monroe said. He put his arm around Cassandra and kissed her cheek.

His wife sighed and leaned into him. "Statistically I think there have to be a lot of unhappily married people in this room to make up for the two pair of happily married at our table and the new bride and groom."

"Sweetie, you're being unusually gloomy."

"No, just a little more realistic than you. One of us occasionally has to keep our feet on the ground."

"My feet haven't been on the ground since the day I met you." Peter stroked his wife's cheek and she smiled at him.

"I'll be the practical one, then."

"I think this is our cue to dance." Clint leaned over and whispered in Laura's ear. She looked at Cassandra and Peter with their heads bent close together.

"Weddings must pull the romantic out of Cassandra."

"Maybe it reminds her of her own wedding."

Laura stepped into his arms. "You're right. If Penelope

and Kyle's nuptials are making me feel warm and fuzzy, they must have had a real strong affect on a couple like Peter and Cassandra."

"What kind of warm and fuzzy feelings?" Clint couldn't help asking.

Laura waited a few seconds and then her eyes met his. "About this morning, I apologize."

He pulled her a little closer, but he wanted more. "And?"

She narrowed her eyes. "And I was the one who initiated last night."

He moved his hand down her back resting it on the small of her back and pulling her lower body snuggly against his. "And?"

"And it was incredible."

"Only incredible? I promise you, I can do better than that."

Her eyes darkened as he brushed a finger along her lower lip. She shivered. "All right, it was better than incredible."

"Oh, no, you're not getting off so easily. You've wounded my manly pride. Now I have to prove to you we can be..."

"What? What can *we* be?" she asked breathlessly, a smile teasing her lips.

He couldn't resist touching her again, wanting to lose himself in the softness of her skin. For one moment he wondered what it would be like if he and Laura really were a married couple dancing together. If he could touch her how he liked, how decency allowed in public, and burning need demanded in private. He was having a good time with her. At the very least he would never be bored. Being with Laura made him...tingly.

Like when he was back home and about to break in a

horse. He got all tingly. So far he had always won, but it was never a given. Especially not with Laura.

He caressed her bare back and Laura rested her head against his shoulder. He continued to move them slowly around the dance floor, his hand stroking her soft skin, smelling the scent of her hair. The music stopped and he reluctantly stepped away from her. Ridiculous. His thoughts were influenced by the case—he'd never been undercover as a married couple with an attractive woman before. That was all. It was nothing to do with the fact that he felt more alive when he was around Laura than anyone else.

Laura and he would never make a good couple.

There might be physical attraction between them, but that was all it was. They were too different, wanted completely different things out of life. Except for the position of homicide detective—they both wanted that job—each for their own reasons. Although their reasons were similar.

He was going home to Two Horse Junction just as soon as Sheriff Conner retired. Then he was going to find himself a nice Texas girl to marry. A gal who wanted a family in a small town.

It was not the life that Laura Carter wanted. Why, she didn't even want to get married. She did not want a family. And she most definitely did not want to live in a hick town like Two Horse Junction. Even he had to admit there would be nothing for an ambitious police officer like herself in Two Horse.

The music had stopped but Laura stood still looking at him. "Maybe you need to show me just how much more incredible we could be together." She stood on her toes and brushed her mouth over his. He stopped himself from hauling her into his arms and showing her exactly how great they would be together...again.

"We could go back to our room." Laura was very pink.

He looked at Peter and Cassandra and saw them still sitting at their table. "We're supposed to be watching Peter's every move."

"We could be fast."

"I like the way you think. But if we're going to be...fast, then there's an empty cloakroom at the end of this hallway."

She raised an eyebrow. "And why have you been staking out cloakrooms?"

"I checked out all the rooms just in case Peter disappeared."

"You are thorough. I like that in a man. I'll meet you there in five minutes."

FOUR AND A HALF minutes later, Clint opened the door to the cloakroom but the room was empty. He stepped in and closed the door behind him. He wiped his hand on his trousers, aware he was just as nervous as when he'd met Mary Jane Polaski behind the barn of the Harvest Dance, hoping to kiss her.

He'd done a lot more than that with Laura, yet it felt like the first time again. Maybe because this time they were planning to make love rather than be surprised by it. He checked his watch.

Not that making out, or whatever they were about to do, was the same as a long romantic dinner, dancing and holding hands, kisses and touches that promised a long night of making love on a comfortable bed.

The cloakroom held a series of racks filled with empty hangers. A kind of rollback shutter door ran across the top half of the front wall, which when open created a window

through which the coats were handed to the coat checker.
Under the counter was a storage space that held a couple
of boxes. At the back of the room was a blue velvet couch,
which he was planning to take advantage of as soon as
Laura arrived.

He checked his watch again. She was five minutes late.
Damn, maybe she'd changed her mind. In fact, now that
he looked around the deserted room, he was beginning to
think suggesting they meet in the cloakroom was a very
bad idea. On the dance floor all he'd wanted to do was
keep her in his arms and make love to her, but making out
in a cloakroom wasn't Laura's style. She wasn't barbecue
and haystacks, she was diamonds and caviar. At the very
least she deserved the big honeymoon bed in their suite.
Clearly she'd come to her senses faster than he had and remembered they were supposed to be undercover as opposed to under the covers.

He'd give her another five minutes—just in case—and
then he'd leave. He could last through the remainder of
the wedding and then he'd take her upstairs and have all
night to make love to her.

And then the case would be over and there would be no
reason for him and Laura to spend any time together.

He looked at his watch again. Laura was fifteen minutes
late; she wasn't meeting him. Still, *we've got tonight* he
thought with anticipation. He had his hand on the doorknob when he heard voices on the other side. He recognized Peter Monroe talking to another man. Their foot-
steps stopped in front of the door and Clint looked for
someplace to hide himself. The storage area under the
counter was the only option.

He managed to stuff himself inside and position the
boxes in front of him. He saw two sets of men's legs enter
the room.

"So we have an agreement then," the stranger said. The voice was a deep baritone and heavily accented.

Vasili.

"It's been a pleasure," Peter agreed. "I wish all my business dealings were this pleasant."

Clint saw the two men lean forward slightly and realized they were shaking hands. He shifted one of the boxes so he could see Peter and the other man.

Peter accepted an envelope from Vasili. "Is this all of it?"

"The last of my donations. For a legitimate businessman you're not bad." Vasili slapped Peter on the shoulder and then the two of them exited, leaving Clint wondering what exactly he had seen.

He waited for the door to the cloakroom to close before he extricated himself from under the counter. He pulled out his gun from the back of his waistband and opened the door to the corridor. No one. He shoved the gun back into its holster and decided to find Laura. If they split up, she could follow Peter and he'd take Vasili. He needed to see inside the envelope the two men had exchanged. Funny, he was actually surprised to see Monroe dealing with Vasili. He liked Peter and had begun to think he might be innocent, that Garrow's information was wrong.

He walked back into the party toward their table. Peter was already back, sitting next to his wife.

"There you are," Cassandra said. "We were beginning to wonder what had happened."

"Where's Laura?" Peter asked.

That was the question. She hadn't met him in the cloakroom and he assumed she had been following Peter. Had Vasili noticed her and done something to Laura? He sat down. "She's freshening up. Did I miss anything?"

"The bride's about to throw the bouquet. Surely Laura doesn't want to miss it."

"She'll be along in a minute," he said. But she wasn't. Peter watched the guests, waving to some acquaintances, leaning in to whisper to his wife. Cassandra smiled at Clint and played with her strand of pearls. "Maybe Laura isn't feeling all that well."

His stomach tightened and he stood up. "I'm going up to our room to check on Laura."

"We'll let her know if she comes back here," Cassandra assured him. A flash of satisfaction shone in her eyes, but she looked away.

Clint weaved his way in and out of the dancing couples to the ballroom doors. Maybe Laura had decided to check on little Petey. To calm his escalating nerves he imagined Laura's reaction to Two Horse Junction. The main street had a diner, Tom's Barber Shop, a bank and The Swann hotel.

The sheriff's office and school were also on the main street. Three streets filled with family homes with large front yards crossed Main Street. The old high school had been converted into apartments housing the few single people in town—a couple of artists and a computer game designer.

Most people, however, were married with families. Which was what Clint wanted for himself. His mother considered weddings and engagements late-breaking news developments that deserved an immediate letter to her eldest son. He knew it was because she wanted him to come home as well. He was certain she'd find Laura completely inappropriate wife material.

His mother would be right.

Laura Carter would take one look at Main Street and turn around on well-shod heels, get back into her BMW and drive away in a cloud of dust. If she ever made it as far as their ranch, she'd look at everything he showed her, the land, the barns, smile that quiet, well-bred smile and make an excuse to leave as quickly as possible. But if he could get her into his big four poster bed with its feather pillows and quilt his grandmother had made and love her until she was too tired to move he could keep her.

Keep her? What in the blazes was he thinking? He didn't want anything more than a fling with Ms. Laura Carter. Ok, maybe, he admitted, after the case was closed, a week on some secluded island where he could ogle her in a bikini and spread sunscreen all over her luscious body would be nice. A week in bed with her would definitely cure him of this incredible fascination he'd developed.

Incredible fascination?

He didn't even like her.

Then why was he always thinking about her? Because she was so different than him. And irritating, in a sexually appealing way of course.

Near the exit of the ballroom the newlyweds were passing out individually wrapped pieces of wedding cake. Penelope waved at him when she saw him and Clint forced himself to stop and kiss her on the cheek. "Thank you so much for coming, Mr. Marshall. Kyle and I really enjoyed spending time with you and Laura. It really helped us to calm our nerves to see how happy you and Laura are. Even when you're so different."

Had she been reading his mind? "Er, yes. Laura and I are very different."

She beamed at him. "Yes. You two make it seem so possible. It made me so sure about marrying Kyle."

"I didn't realize you were having doubts."

Penelope waved at someone in the crowd. "Every bride has some doubts. Marriage is a leap of faith in what the two of you can do together. You and Laura showed me that it can work. If it had only been Peter and Cassandra Monroe on the yacht, I'm not sure I would have walked down the aisle. Peter and Cassandra should be doing so well together, yet..." she shrugged.

"What do you mean?"

"Never mind my wedding day jitters. Here I am blathering on like I'm an expert on marriage and I've been married for a grand total of four hours." She giggled and handed him two pieces of wedding cake. "Where is Laura?"

"She went to check on our son." He quashed the feeling of how right the words felt. He took her hand in his and squeezed. "All our very best wishes for your life together. Kyle is a lucky young man."

The bride turned to gaze fondly on her new husband. "Yes, he is. Oh, there are the Buckholts, I have to go say hello."

Clint made his way to the elevator and to their honeymoon suite, feeling almost as nervous as a groom. Because he was worried about where Laura had disappeared to, that was it. No other reason whatsoever.

He unlocked the door and stepped inside. The hotel baby-sitter looked up from the couch and put down the magazine she was reading. "You're back early. The baby is fine. I just checked on him. Someone named Amber called as well to say she's feeling safe and wanted to know if she could come by tomorrow morning for her property. Where's Mrs. Marshall?"

"I thought she might be here." If she wasn't here, then where the hell could she be?

"She came by about a half hour ago to check on Petey. Then a bellboy delivered a note and she said she had to get back to the wedding."

"What note?"

"She took it with her. But she said she had to meet someone."

"She didn't say she was going to find me first?"

"No. She didn't leave you a message."

Clint didn't like this. Laura could be in trouble and he had no idea where she was. "Did you see what direction she headed in?"

The woman was gathering her magazines. "Out the door, that's all I know. She got the note and she couldn't get out of here fast enough. Listen, if you're back for the night I'll just get you to sign my chit and—"

"I can't stay." He heard something rip and looked down to see Sweetums pulling on his pant leg. The dog had ripped and drooled on the previously immaculate cuffs of his tuxedo pants. She sat back on her haunches and looked at him with adoration. "I don't have time for you now."

He opened the door and turned back to the baby-sitter. "If Laura comes by tell her I'm looking for her and she should stay here. I have my cell phone. She can call me."

He stepped out and felt something attached to his leg. "Sweetums, we don't have time to play games right now." He unhooked the dog from his leg and scooped her back into the room. She looked at him adoringly. He closed the door and turned toward the elevator and almost tripped over the small bundle of fluff.

He scooped Sweetums into his arms. "Don't be ridiculous, you can't come with me." The dog looked at him and then looked down the hallway and Clint finally understood what the dog was trying to tell him. "You're looking for Laura, too, aren't you? Well don't worry, I'm going to find her. Just as soon as I get you locked up in our room."

Sweetums raised her ears and growled at him. She jumped out of his arms and headed toward the fire exit. At the door she looked back at Clint and drooled.

"I've got to be crazy," Clint said as he followed the dog.

10

SWEETUMS JUMPED step by step down four stairs and then stopped. She sniffed the ground, turned in a circle and sniffed at the floor again. She looked at Clint and blinked. "Which way, Lassie?" he asked. "Up or down?"

Sweetums scowled, baring her teeny teeth at him and shook her head, her pink bow flapping disdainfully at him. She jumped back up a step, then a second and a third and back to the landing where Clint was standing. Again, she sniffed the floor, seemed to roll back her shoulders in determination and began to tackle the stairs. Clint watched her take each stair with slow and steady deliberation. When she finished mounting a half-dozen steps she sat down and panted, then began again.

Clint sighed. "This is ridiculous. At this pace you'll take all night. A Texas coyote would have had you scooped up in its mouth and had you as an appetizer before you even had time to think about running away." Sweetums looked back at him once and then resumed her climb.

Clint took the steps she had conquered in three big strides and picked her up, carrying her to the next floor, the twenty-second. He put her down, she sniffed and then pointed at the stairs with her head. "Okay boss, up we go." He picked her up again and they repeated this process until they reached the thirtieth floor. This time Sweetums pawed at the door, wanting in to the hallway.

Hardly able to believe he was following a lapdog's lead,

he opened the door and she scurried down the hallway stopping at every door. She crisscrossed back and forth, going back to a door she had already investigated and then hurrying ahead three doors. "This is the last floor of the hotel and you're just making this look good aren't you?" he demanded, trying to ignore the growing feeling of dread. Where was Laura? Was she in some kind of danger? He glared at Sweetums who ignored him. "Of course I've started talking to a dog and I'm following you thinking you're some kind of miniature Lassie." Deciding he was absolutely ridiculous and should head back to the hotel room, he leaned down to pick up Sweetums, who scurried away with an excited yip. "Come back you silly bundle of fluff, the time for games is over."

Sweetums, however, continued to run, and stopped in front of the Royal Suite. She sat back on her hind legs and drooled. Clint was just about to pick her up and take her back to their suite when he remembered the Royal Suite was where Cassandra and Peter were staying.

Sweetums pawed at the door, whimpered and then looked at him.

"If you're wrong I'm going to look really stupid about this. I'll take you to Texas and feed you to the coyotes personally."

Sweetums bared her teeth at him and knocked the door with her head.

"Okay, I get the message. You think Laura is here." He knocked on the door and waited for an answer. When no one answered he looked up and down the hallway, pulled a set of lock picks from inside his jacket and hunched over the door.

The Regal was an old-fashioned hotel, proud of its heritage, which luckily meant the doors still had keys and keyholes as opposed to the electronic cards. He'd learnt a fair bit from his fellow officers in Dallas, especially Eddie Harte, a former criminal delinquent. Eddie had taught Clint the basics of picking locks and Clint put his skills to use.

It took him longer than Eddie would have liked, but Clint finally got the lock open and he entered the suite. The front room of the luxury suite was a living room with blue velvet couches and wing chairs covered in blue and yellow French Provençal fabric. To the right was a dining room that could seat twenty. Had the Monroes really had occasion to host a large dinner party in their suite? Beyond the dining room was an office complete with fax, television and Internet access. The corridor on the other side of the living room led to three bedrooms, but Laura was nowhere to be found. He checked the closets and bathrooms in each bedroom feeling more and more ridiculous as he went. Still no Laura.

He went back to the living room where Sweetums had curled up on one of the velvet couches. "Get off," he said as he picked up the idiot ball of fluff, "You've shed all over the damn couch. They'll know right away someone was here, and it won't take a rocket scientist to figure out it was you." He placed Sweetums on the floor and tried to brush the strands of dog fur off the couch but they stubbornly clung to the velvet. Damn, he didn't have time for this. Nevertheless, he began to use his fingers to pick up each strand of fur individually. After several minutes he stood back to see if it would pass casual observation. The couch still looked like a dog had been shedding over it. "I can't believe you shed that much fur in five minutes."

Needing to get out of the empty suite before Peter or Cassandra returned to find him burgling their rooms, he decided to turn over the cushion and hope for the best. As he picked up the cushion something fell to the floor.

"Damn." Bending down to pick it up, his breath caught in his chest.

It was a diamond and sapphire earring, one he had watched Laura put on earlier that evening.

Sweetums growled and tugged on his much-mangled trouser leg with her teeth.

The nervous feeling was overtaken by dread. Laura had been here. "Okay, I give up," he told the dog. "You were right. Where is she?"

Sweetums scurried across the dining room and began to sniff along the walls. Trying to belie the tension, Clint leaned against the doorframe and waited. At the very least he knew when to defer to a better detective than himself. He concentrated on the dog, not on the images of an injured Laura that ran through his mind. He was going to find her and she was going to be all right.

Sweetums circled the room twice before stopping in front of a large painting of a fox hunt. She sat down on her haunches and stared at it. Clint joined her. A very badly painted picture of British aristocrats and their dogs and horses suited the Regal's personality. To the right he noticed a button and pushed it. The painting swung aside to reveal a dumb waiter.

"Of course. This is how you got food to the dining room for very private functions. No servants required to see what was going on." He found the knob and pulled the door open.

Inside lay a crumpled Laura.

Unable to tell if she was conscious or not, he squeezed his hands into the cramped space and pulled her out trying to cushion her with his arms so that she wouldn't hurt herself against the walls.

Once he had pulled her most of the way out of the cramped space he felt her move slightly so that she was able to push with her feet to get completely out. When he had her standing upright, he clutched her against his chest. She felt so damn good in his arms he thought as he inhaled the scent of her hair and waited for his racing heart to calm. Finally, Laura made some kind of noise and Clint realized he was suffocating her. "Sorry." Still keeping his hands on her shoulders he looked at her. Her arms were bound behind her back, her legs tied together and her mouth taped. Reaching out, he took a corner of the tape and ripped it off her mouth.

"Ouch." She turned around. "Untie my hands first, I swear my left arm fell asleep about an hour ago."

He noted the expert knots binding her wrists together and untied her. She leaned forward to loosen her feet, but he brushed her aside. "Let me help you." She stretched her arms over her head.

"Do you have the knots? I can do this."

"Be still, it won't kill you to let someone else help you."

"I'm such an idiot," Laura grumbled. "I was distracted because I was going to meet you, I was thinking about that."

"The baby-sitter said you received a note?" he asked.

"It was from you, saying you wanted to meet in the Monroes' suite. I thought that you'd found something about the case. The hotel door was partly open when I got here so I walked in like an idiot. I never saw the person who hit me over the head. The next thing I knew I woke up in that tiny box. How did you find me?"

"Sweetums found you."

"Sweetums?" The look on his face must have confirmed his words because she picked up the little dog and kissed her on the top of her head. Clint wished she'd done the same to him.

"So you were coming to meet me," he prodded, "then what happened?"

"I saw Peter and Nicholas Vasili coming out of the cloakroom. It was too late to turn around, plus I wondered how Peter would react when I saw him with Nicholas, so I kept going forward. Peter introduced Vasili to me and explained they were doing some work together." She frowned and scratched Sweetum's head. "It was funny. It really was as if he had nothing to hide."

"I heard Peter and Vasili finishing their business deal while I was hiding in the cloakroom."

"So you were there."

"Of course I was. I never saw you when I left the room, what happened?"

"I had said goodbye to Peter and Vasili, neither of whom were the slightest bit concerned that I had seen them together—" Laura shook her head and Sweetums nuzzled her neck. "—anyway Peter went back into the wedding reception and Nicholas disappeared into an elevator. I decided to check on Petey and that's when I got the note. What the heck was I crammed into?"

"It's the dumbwaiter."

Either Peter or Vasili could have arranged to have Laura ambushed. They needed to tell Garrow what had happened. "Someone knows we're investigating Peter."

He heard the door to the suite open. Taking Laura's arm he pointed to the door leading to the den. They crept inside the room and Clint opened the door to the closet. "What is it with you and small spaces?" Laura muttered. He stepped in first and she followed leaving the door open a half inch or so. As he had hoped, Peter walked into the study.

Laura stiffened and touched his arm as Peter pulled out

the envelope from his jacket, took out a stack of money and documents.

"Bingo."

They were out of the closet simultaneously. Clint aimed his revolver at Monroe. "Hold it right there. You're under arrest."

Peter dropped the money and he looked uncertainly from Clint to Laura and back to Clint again. He smiled weakly as he pointed at the gun in Clint's hand. "You'd better watch that, it looks very real. How did you two get in here? What kind of a joke is this?"

"This is no joke, in fact you're going to be very sorry you ever met us." Clint pulled out his handcuffs.

Peter's gaze wavered as he looked at the cuffs. Clint handed his gun to Laura, grabbed Monroe's hands and cuffed him. "My God, you're after the money." He nodded toward the table. "Go ahead. Take it. There's over two hundred thousand dollars there."

"We're not after your money," Laura said. "We're police officers. Damn, my badge is in my purse. Clint show him your ID."

Clint pulled out his badge. Peter read it and paled. "What in the world am I under arrest for?"

"Try kidnapping for one." Laura rubbed the sore bump against her forehead. "And consorting with a known criminal."

"You mean Nicholas Vasili. I can explain—"

"Go ahead and explain it to the judge. Special Financial Investigations has been after you for a long time. Now that they finally have your money laundering connections in the open they're going to be able to track every—"

"Money laundering. What are you talking about? That money was part of my deal with Vasili—for a baby!" A fine line of sweat had broken out across Monroe's forehead.

"What?"

Peter turned to Clint, his face pleading. "I know it's wrong, but what's the point in having all this money if I can't have the one thing I want most in my life, a family? Cassandra and I aren't able to have children and the adoption process is long and well, for the first time ever Cassandra started talking about how much she wanted a baby, and I grabbed the opportunity. Vasili said he could cut through all the Russian red tape and get us a baby in a week if I was willing to pay for it." He turned red but he continued. "I know it was wrong, but I decided to use what I had and start my family."

Laura wished she could believe him. "If you're buying a baby then why do you have Vasili's money? He should have your money."

Monroe's face paled as he looked at the money and licked his lips. "It was a two-part deal. He does a favor for me and I do one for him. It seemed harmless enough."

"Laundering money is harmless?"

"I was giving Vasili's money to a charity. It's a Russian adoption group, a legitimate organization, not the source he uses for people like me who are in a hurry to get a baby. They refuse to take his money." He shrugged. "They'll take mine. I am paying for the baby with a donation to the charity, but Vasili wanted to give them more money. I give them the money and receive a nice tax receipt. It seemed like a good deal at the time."

Laura looked at Clint and touched him on the arm. "What if what he's saying is true?"

"The court can decide that."

"He's got a damn good story. Don't you think all of this

is just a little convenient? Every time we need to find
something incriminating about Peter we do?"

Clint hated to admit it but the same niggling doubt had
been worrying him as well. The evidence against Monroe
was practically thrown their way. The documents on the
boat, now this.

Laura flushed a delightful shade of pink. "The note I received was quite intimate..." She shot a look at Peter.
"How did you know that I was having doubts about Clint
and me and wanted to be reassured?"

"What are you talking about? I thought you two were
happily married."

"We're cops," she reminded him. "The fulfillment of
your ideal. The cowboy and the princess."

"Why, yes." Peter considered them as if he hadn't seen
them clearly before. "Cowboy and establishment. I admire both those aspects of America."

"You were supposed to. How did you know what to
write to send me to rushing to meet Clint?"

"I don't know what you're talking about," he protested.
"Except for the blackmarket baby I've had nothing to do
with Vasili. I only met him for the first time last week."

Peter Monroe shook his head. "I realize this looks bad,
but all of my dealings with Nicholas Vasili have been re-
cent. A friend of mine adopted a child through Vasili and
told me about him and the deal. We only met last week.
He said we could finalize the deal in Chicago so I had him
invited to the wedding so we could meet without attracting any suspicion. Some criminal I turned out to be. But
you said you've been investigating me for months. That
doesn't make any sense. Why have people been investigating me? Why did you bring your son along with you
on this case?"

"We're not a couple and he's not our son."

"Not a couple? Huh, if any two people were meant to be together I thought it was you two. But you've got the wrong man, all of my business dealings have been aboveboard. The only dishonest transaction I've ever made is trying to buy a child. If you take me in, I'll never be able to close this deal with Vasili."

"That's exactly the idea," Laura said. But like Clint she didn't move. "Clint, this is very strange. My gut is telling me that Peter is being set up."

"I agree. But Garrow knows that the Russian money definitely went through Monroe's company. If it's not Peter, then someone is setting him up."

"Impossible, I don't have Russian Mafia money in my company."

"Yes, you do." Laura said. "SFI has known about the money for some time. They haven't been able to connect it directly to you."

"They won't be able to," Peter sputtered. "I made millions on my own. Why would I need to launder money? I wouldn't risk everything I've built. There has to be some mistake."

"I'm afraid you're the one making the mistake—again," a voice from the doorway said.

"I should have known." Laura felt the missing pieces fall into place as Cassandra Monroe entered the room, a semiautomatic pistol pointed at them.

Peter's mouth opened but nothing came out as he stared at his wife. His eyes flickered between the gun and his wife's face. "Cassie, what's the meaning of this?" he demanded in a tight voice.

"Cassandra. God I always hated it when you shortened my name. But that was just another thing you never knew about me, did you? My dear sweet husband."

Peter flinched at his wife's words, stepping toward her.

"I'd stop right there, unless you want to be the first to be shot." Peter halted in his tracks. Cassandra smiled at the look on his face. "The meaning of all this, my dear sweet husband, is that you've performed all the steps of my dance very well, with only a slight miscalculation at the end. You two," she indicated Clint and Laura. "If you had only arrested Peter and taken Vasili's money as evidence, it would have been perfect. You could have locked him up and thrown away the key. But I had a bad feeling about the two of you ever since I figured out you were undercover cops." She smiled. "I admit you had me fooled at first with that cowboy-and-heiress-with-a-stupid-dog routine. I never thought the police department had so much imagination. But once I learned Agent Garrow had placed someone in the wedding, I realized it had to be my husband's new best friends. Really Peter you were so gullible."

"How did you know that Agent Garrow had placed operatives inside the York-Chandler wedding?" Clint asked.

"As soon as I knew SFI had taken my bait and was investigating Peter, I made it my business to find someone in the department who liked to talk about what was going on. My private investigator made friends with a chatty secretary who tried to impress him with information about the different cases. I have to admit even I was surprised at how many investigations operated at any one point."

Laura finally understood just how much Cassandra had hated being Peter's wife. "And you were the one who originally tipped off SFI about Peter's supposed criminal activities. Wouldn't it have been simpler to get a divorce?"

Cassandra smiled genuinely. "I needed to make my own fortune. I've grown accustomed to living well and

Vasili paid well, really well. And there was the added fun of making Peter the fall guy. Sending SFI an anonymous tip was easy as I was revealing my own plans. And it was all working so well, until the pair of you showed up and began to wonder about why Peter had so willingly walked into your trap. It's a shame really. If you had arrested Peter and taken him to the police station, you'd be perfectly safe. And I could have played the distraught wife very convincingly."

"When we questioned you about Peter's business and his associates you would have incriminated Peter even further," Laura said.

"Exactly." Cassandra smiled. "By the time Peter was convicted I planned to be both a celebrity as the poor deceived wife who took over her husband's business and a successful executive who took over her husband's company."

Peter was staring at his wife like he'd never seen her before. "But I loved you. How could you?"

"You took several business calls on our honeymoon. That's when I knew I'd made a mistake marrying you and decided to use our marriage to my advantage."

"But how did you launder Vasili's money? SFI could never understand why so many different divisions were involved," Laura asked, trying to buy them time. Now that Cassandra was finally revealing her real self, her ego wanted to boast of her accomplishments, giving Laura and Clint time to figure out how to disarm her.

"I established warm relations with several of my dear husband's vice presidents. The average vice president in Monroe Industries is fifty-two years old and spends at least sixty hours a week at the office. When he sees me, when I begin to flirt, it's like I've brought his youth back. Most of them were only too eager to fall into my bed—and then to help me move some money around so that I'd be able to divorce Peter. Of course, by the time he realized he'd been had, he was guilty of money laundering and of having an affair with the boss's wife. He kept quiet. I moved on to the next candidate."

Laura was shocked by the woman's cold-bloodedness. "That's why SFI was never able to make any connections to Peter. You were the common denominator. And the men you duped."

"Exactly," Cassandra agreed. "I was afraid you might be the weak spot in my plan. You seemed to understand right away how frustrated I was."

Laura ignored her words. Peter stepped toward his wife. "Cassandra, whatever this is about, it's not too late. I can help you work this out—"

"Don't take another step toward me. I don't want your hands on me ever again."

Peter's complexion paled and he stopped dead in his tracks.

Laura looked at Clint and saw that he had moved about a foot to the left. She continued to inch to the right. *Keep talking* she tried to mentally tell Peter. With her husband distracting her, either she or Clint might be able to jump Cassandra and disarm her. She took another small step.

"Cassandra, I love you. I didn't tell you why I kept ducking out for meetings during the wedding, I know how crazy that made you, but I was getting us a baby. Just picture it—you and me and a child. We'd be a real family."

"And you thought I would be happy taking care of a smelly infant." Cassandra sneered. "Really, you never did learn the first thing about me. I have no desire to take care of a crying, spewing infant."

"But you liked their baby, little Petey."

"Don't be ridiculous. I let you think I found the child tolerable so Vasili's baby deal would appeal to you. I needed you to negotiate the baby deal with him and agree to take his stupid charity money so that our two detectives could catch you red-handed in a deal with the Russian Mafia. They would never have believed your baby story and you would have gone to jail for a very long time."

She smiled fondly, then aimed her gun at Clint. "Now if you and Laura don't stand perfectly still I'll be forced to shoot one of you. Mr. Cowboy would be my first choice. My associate will handle Laura."

Laura felt the cold steel press against the back of her neck and froze.

"I can't believe this," Peter said. "Tom. You're involved in this. With my wife?"

The man behind Laura said, "Your wife made me a proposition I was unable to turn down. She is a very remarkable woman."

Peter turned a defeated face toward Laura. "You saw Tom Watson at the boat. He's the Vice President of Legal Affairs."

"Cassandra is a remarkable woman. She's shown me a whole new world of possibilities. I'm only sorry that it's going to turn out so badly for you. Although I don't think you would have liked jail very much."

"I trusted you—and Cassandra." Peter's brow crinkled as if he were fighting off a headache. Laura thought his eyes looked a little misty. Had he really loved his wife that much? It just went to prove her theory that marriage brought you grief even if you continued to stay in love. Look at Peter Monroe. His love for Cassandra had blinded him to her activities. "How long has this been going on?" Peter asked tiredly.

Tom took the gun away from Laura's neck and she took

in a deep breath. He stood next to her and grinned. "We've been involved for about two years. The moment I met her at the executive brunch at your home I knew I had found the woman of my dreams."

Cassandra looked at her lover fondly, although not with love, Laura noted. She wondered how long Cassandra intended to keep Tom around once his usefulness had been fully milked. "I had been looking for a man like Tom all my life. A man who saw more in me than my beauty."

"I always saw a lot more to you than your looks. I loved you," Peter said.

Cassandra harrumphed. "You fell in love with my beauty and what you thought I was—the dutiful corporate daughter who would make the perfect corporate wife. But whenever I tried to talk to you about your business negotiations or offer you any advice you wouldn't listen to me."

"If you had wanted to develop your own business I would have supported you. I only wanted you to be happy. I loved you but I never agreed with your advice when it came to my company."

"You never gave me a chance so I decided to create my own opportunity."

"By stealing from me and having me sent to jail?"

"Yes." Cassandra motioned for Tom to move Clint and Laura next to her husband. Tom uncuffed Peter's hands. "Too bad these two had to ruin that plan. Now I'm afraid the three of you are going to meet a very unpleasant end. Peter and Clint are going to fatally shoot each other." She turned her gun on Laura. "You are going to get caught in the crossfire."

Clint felt his stomach plummet as Cassandra held her gun on Laura. He stepped in front of Laura, protecting her with his body. He always protected his partner.

"Still playing the protective lover," Cassandra snarled. "It's not going to do you any good. I'm just as happy to shoot you first. What the—" She shook her foot. "Damn, your stupid dog is slobbering all over my alligator shoes. Really, I don't know how you can stand that irritating drooler."

She leaned in closer, pressed her gun against Clint's chest and whispered, "You've got it real bad for Laura. Too bad you never had the chance to tell her you love her."

He jerked his head in surprise.

"I know your type," she continued. "You don't say what you feel until you've had time to work it out—and then only because you're planning a proposal of marriage. She would never marry you. But she's sure knocked you off your well-ordered world."

No, he didn't love Laura. It was just nerves. The natural reaction of a man facing his possible end with the woman he'd spent a number of incredible days with. His hormones and his natural impulse to feel something for the woman he bedded was just playing with his mind.

He didn't like Laura Carter very much. She annoyed him and got under his skin and challenged him and refused to back down. While she was driven and was more interested in proving herself to the rest of the world than in making him happy, she *did* make him happy. He liked the way she had adapted whenever their assignment had changed, including taking care of Amber's child.

For a woman who claimed not to want a family she'd taken to Petey like a natural. She made one hell of a lover. If she ever decided she wanted more than a job, she'd make a great mother, too.

They may only have spent a few days together but he understood Laura better than anyone he'd ever met before. He understood her desire to prove that she was the best, that she deserved to be a homicide detective. He liked her courage and her independence. From what she'd said of her family, he'd learned that she needed all of her guts to stand up to her disapproving mother. He'd love to give that woman a piece of his mind about her treatment of Laura. How could the woman not see what a treasure she had in her daughter?

Ice princess were the last words he'd use to describe Laura now that he'd gotten to know her. She was passionate, brave, funny and very much all woman.

Tom Watson bent down and scooped Sweetums into his arms. The dog tried to wiggle out of his arms, but when Watson kept the dog clamped tight against his chest Sweetums sunk her teeth into his arm.

Watson screamed, dropping the dog and his gun. Annoyed by the dog, Cassandra whirled around, aiming her gun at Sweetums. "Get away from that damn dog. I'm going to shoot it."

"No," Tom answered. "It's just a dog."

Clint threw himself on Cassandra, tackling her to the ground. He managed to grab the hand holding the gun and slammed it against the floor making her drop the weapon. She raked her fingernails across his face and fought against him with strength but he wrestled her down, capturing her flailing arms, finally holding her still. He dragged her upright and Laura pressed her gun against Cassandra's temple.

Peter was holding a gun on Tom Watson. Sweetums ran back and forth at the activity, first drooling on Clint, running over to Peter and then back to Clint. Then the silly heroic dog sat down on her back haunches and began to bark, louder and louder.

"Oh, my. Sweetums is better. She can bark!" Laura

burst into tears. "You're such a good dog. You are the most brilliant dog in the entire world."

Clint looked at her cuddling Sweetums, tears streaking her face. He had been so wrong about her. She'd never been an ice princess.

And he was in love with her.

11

HECK, THAT SURE WAS FUN pretending to be married. Want to do it for real and move to Two Horse Junction? Clint could picture Laura's polite and chilled reaction as she tried to let him down gently.

Clint wondered if everyone knew how in love he was with Laura. What did his mother always say—there was no point in pretending to have feelings that weren't there. He should just out and tell Laura. Somehow he thought a mule kicking him in the head might feel better than telling Laura a cowpoke from Two Horse Junction was in love with her. She'd consider it a good joke.

"Come on," Laura touched his arm, "Let's go to the precinct and fill out the paperwork. I have a dog I have to take home." Garrow had taken Petey to the SFI offices so that Captain Clark wouldn't see Amber picking up her child, saving Clint and Laura from the complicated explanations.

Feeling peculiar, wondering exactly when he had lost grip on reality, Clint drove the red sports car back to the station. It had only been four days since he'd picked her up at her apartment. Laura and the silly, heroic bundle of fluff she considered a dog. Sweetums sat in Laura's lap, a pink bow adorning her head. Sweetums turned toward him and drooled. Laura never turned once to look at him, although he spent a considerable amount of time stealing glances at her. As much as he liked looking at her legs, he was more concerned with her suddenly cool demeanor.

"Are you all right?" he asked.

"Fine," she replied. "I'm fine." Her blue eyes met his and then she looked back out the window of the car. "Why wouldn't I be fine?"

"The case."

She patted Sweetums. "The case went well. We got an arrest. I think Garrow is going to get a conviction. He's very determined. If anyone can follow Cassandra's paper trail, it will be him."

He wanted her to ask the question women always asked: will I see you again? What about us? Laura, of course, did nothing of the kind. "I guess you'll be happy to get back to your regular life," he said.

"Of course," she answered. "My regular life."

Her life that did not include him. He tried to imagine having dinner with Laura's mother. She would take one look at him and shudder. Nor could he imagine making small talk with her banker cousins. Unless of course he wanted to share how his daddy had stolen the life savings of most people in Two Horse Junction. He didn't fit into her life and she wouldn't fit into his.

His parents' marriage had taught him the folly of that. They'd loved one another—he didn't doubt that for a moment—but his father had never been satisfied with life in a two horse town. And his mother had found the bigger cities and the constant moving distressing. She had wanted a family and roots.

Elizabeth Marshall had been able to stand proud every time her husband left because she was sure he was coming back. Besides which, she had a family to raise. But her husband's larceny had almost been too much for her. Clint remembered the month she refused to leave the house, the many days she had refused to get out of bed. On those days he had woken up his brothers, made them toast for breakfast, gotten them all to school with firm instructions not to say a word about Mama and lived through the schoolyard taunts about their father.

He had vowed to never be his father—to never repeat his father's mistakes. Falling in love with Laura, imagining they could have any kind of life together, was exactly what his father would have done.

"We're here," Laura said. "Is something wrong?"

"Wrong? No." Clint realized he had pulled into their precinct's parking lot and had already turned off the engine. "I was just thinking about the case."

"About which one of us might be promoted?" Laura asked.

"No. I hadn't thought about that for a couple of days." He undid his seat belt and turned to her. "Listen, Laura. About what happened between us—"

She pulled her hands out of his, he hadn't realized he'd reached for her. "Don't worry about it—us. It was just a fling. We were stuck together and being a man and a woman well...things just happened." She stumbled over her words as she reached for the door handle and opened it.

He watched her escape and slammed his hand against the steering wheel. What did he expect her to say—that she'd been so overwhelmed by his lovemaking that she'd fallen in love with him and wanted to follow him back to Two Horse? He got out of the car and followed her into the station.

Captain Clark was waiting for them. He clapped Clint on the shoulder and nodded in Laura's direction. "Didn't think you two would pull this off, especially without killing each other. The cowboy and the heiress." He laughed.

"Best joke we ever had." He noticed Sweetums in Laura's arms. "What's that?"

"That's Laura's dog, she was very useful to us in the case."

Captain Clark stepped closer to stare at Sweetums. "That's a dog? Carter, you're even stranger than I thought. Well, what are you two standing around here for? There are other cases to be solved. We're not about to throw you a ticker tape parade."

"Aye, aye, boss," Clint saluted but both Clark and Laura ignored him. He went to his own desk, all the time aware of what Laura was doing.

Laura skimmed through her in-tray while Sweetums sat on her desk. The dog looked around the cluttered office and shook her head in disgust. She looked questioningly at Clint and then lay down covering her eyes with her paws and went to sleep.

Stan Lesky sidled up to Clint while he was checking his voicemail. He wanted to call Amber and tell her that Garrow had arranged to have Petey looked after in his office. They had agreed the upscale, quiet SFI offices were a better place for the child—and Garrow could pretend Petey was his nephew. He'd also volunteered to look after the baby if Amber wasn't able to come for him today. Clint was sure he could find her a legitimate job if she hadn't already found one for herself.

When he hung up the phone Laura walked over to him. "I'm going to take Sweetums home. She's been through a lot."

He stood and wished Lesky would leave so he could talk to Laura in private. "Give her an extra dog biscuit from me."

"Are you kidding, she's set for doggy biscuits for life after saving us." She looked down at her feet, then at her fidgeting hands. "I wanted to say...uh, that it was well...well," she took a deep breath, "a pleasure working with you."

"Yeah, we got along better than spikes on a cactus."

Laura frowned. "Hmm, yes." She held out her hand. "I learned a lot. Maybe we'll be teamed up again sometime."

"You never know." He smiled coolly, afraid everyone in the station house could see how crazy head over heels he was about Laura Carter.

She looked like she wanted to say something else, but she turned on her heel and left.

"Wow, man, that's some caboose on that woman. Did you get to play trains with her?" Lesky asked.

"As always your lack of subtlety is amazing. Officer Carter and I worked together on a case, that's it."

"The ice princess froze you out. I'm not surprised."

"She's a good cop. That's all that's important." He stood up and threw his case folder on his desk. "You're all idiots."

LAURA PUT ON her favorite nightgown, a soft yellow silk gown that skimmed along her body and made her feel feminine and slightly wicked. What would Clint think if he saw her in this? With any luck he'd throw her over his shoulder and haul her into the bedroom where she'd make his toes curl in his cowboy boots.

She shook her head. She had spent too much time with the cowboy. Or maybe it had been too long since she'd admitted she wanted a lover.

She stared at her toes and decided to paint her nails. She chose Passion in Pink from her large assortment of colors—whenever she was stressed she bought herself a new nail polish and lipstick—sat down on her couch, placed a box of chocolate truffles on the coffee table in front of her and uncapped the nail polish bottle. With swift strokes she began to paint her toenails.

She imagined Clint holding her foot, brushing the color on her nails, then his hands stroking along the inside of her foot, around her ankle up her calf...

She slammed the top back on the bottle, flopped back against the couch and hugged a pillow to herself. What was wrong with her? Why couldn't she stop thinking about that stupid Neanderthal cowboy?

Because he got her all hot and bothered and they hadn't been able to douse that fire. Clint had kissed her and made her want him again—but they hadn't made it to bed a second time. If only they could have spent a week together, maybe on a beach somewhere, with the sun warming their bodies and the sand cushioning them as they made love.... Laura shook her head.

She was afraid that she would be spending even more time fantasizing about Clint than before he'd touched her.

She thought about changing into a short, sexy dress and driving over to Clint's apartment. Maybe the blue dress—he'd seemed to like it when he'd picked her up to take her to the hotel.

What if she hadn't been anything more than an amusement while he was assigned to a boring case?

She sighed and hugged the pillow more closely to her. *Face it*, she thought. *You don't have the guts to put on a short, sexy dress and drive over to Clint's apartment and seduce him.*

Sure, they'd had a good time together. She'd had a better time with him than she had with anyone. He understood the way she thought. She'd liked spending time with him—killing time. And the sex. Well, that had been just about perfect.

A good-looking man.

Fun times.

Perfect sex.

So why was she sitting on the couch, alone? Why wasn't she willing to take a risk and go after him? Tell him that she would like to be with him...for a while. She didn't have any delusions that their attraction was anything more than a case of opposites attracting, but attract her he did. And she didn't want to stop so soon. They could have fun together.

She'd heard the department erupt in laughter as soon as she had exited the station room. Another joke about the ice princess. She'd stood in the hallway for a moment, waiting to see if Clint might follow her, to check on Sweetums or maybe herself. After all, they had almost been killed today. Instead Clint had stayed with the guys and had joined in with them making fun of her.

Sweetums jumped on the couch next to her, nudging the pillow aside and putting her head on Laura's lap. She scratched the dog behind her ears and her tail wagged up and down on the couch in ecstasy. "Do you miss little Petey as well?" Laura wished she could have looked after the baby for a few more days. Somehow she'd been so overwhelmed by Clint that without him and Petey she felt lonely. Which was ridiculous because she liked being alone.

She missed Petey.

Continuing to scratch the dog's ears, she crooned, "You are a brave and brilliant dog. You saved us all today. Tomorrow we'll go shopping and buy you the biggest, shiniest bow and a cashmere sweater." Sweetums raised her head and growled. "Unless you want something in leather. Now that you're a tough life-saving dog, maybe you should dress in black leather."

Sweetums drooled appreciatively and Laura grabbed some tissues before the doggie spit ended up all over her yellow peignoir. She wiped Sweetums's mouth just as the dog jumped off the couch and headed toward the door. She got to it and sniffed. She looked back at Laura and barked.

"Sssh, darling, you'll wake up the neighbors."

Sweetums continued to bark, her pitch growing higher and faster. Laura hurried to the door. Sweetums had turned her head back to Laura and barked encouragingly. She scooped the dog up into her arms. "I'm glad you got your voice back, and at the most opportune time, but there's no one at the door. See I'll show you." She opened the door. And gasped.

"It's you," she said stupidly.

"It sure is." Clint tipped back his cowboy hat and grinned at her. "I thought this little one was going to pull down the roof with all that commotion."

"I guess she smelled your scent outside the door."

He leaned forward and patted the dog. "She was a real hero today."

"Yes." She stared at him. He looked delicious in a worn tanned leather jacket, jeans and cowboy boots.

"Can I come in?"

"What? Of course, come in. You just surprised me, I wasn't expecting—"

Clint walked into her living room looking at the beige couch, vanilla colored carpet and her overstuffed cream-colored chair. "You sure do like white."

"It's various shades of white—vanilla, cream, cloud." He was right, it was all white—to match the ice princess.

As if he realized he'd said the wrong thing, he smiled. "I sure do like your nightgown. It's sexy." He took a step closer to her and her breath caught in her throat.

"Why did you come? The case is over." Why couldn't

she say she was happy to see him? That she wished they could try and be friends and maybe lovers. To see if...

She remembered the laughter from the precinct and remembered why she protected herself. She always fell for the wrong kind of men. Clint might not be a fortune hunter or liar, but she was behaving ridiculously in thinking they could have any kind of future together. Not only were they competing for the same job, but he intended to head back to Seven Goat Watering Hole as soon as he could. Find himself a sweet hometown girl who would be happy baking pies and looking after babies.

For a second she imagined holding Clint's baby in her arms and she melted.

Clint took another step closer to her. "I came by because we had a date."

"A date?"

"In a cloakroom, no less." He took another step closer. "I thought your apartment might be a little bit more comfortable."

"My apartment is completely beige. Cold."

He moved closer still. "But *you're* not cold. You make me burn every time I look at you."

"I do?" She gulped.

"I missed you." He touched her cheek with his hand, ran his finger down her face to her neck.

"It's only been a few hours." Her mouth fell open as his thumb stroked her bottom lip. From somewhere deep inside she gathered her courage. She needed to tell Clint how important he was to her.

"Five hours. The entire time I was thinking about your lips and what it would be like to kiss you." He lowered his head and kissed her, his mouth gentle.

She gasped for breath when he broke their kiss. "I was

sitting here tonight, wishing I had the nerve to show up at your apartment."

"You don't know where I live."

"Hey! I'm a cop, a pretty good one. I would have found out where you lived." She leaned in a couple of inches and inhaled the smell of him. "Will you stay tonight?"

"Try and kick me out," he scooped her up into his arms. "Which way?"

"Straight down the hallway." She giggled as he headed toward her bedroom.

"What's so funny?" he asked.

She nibbled on his ear. "I imagined you carrying me to the bedroom, but not this elegantly."

"You mean like this?" Clint twisted her in his arms and before she knew what had happened she was staring at the floor, her derriere in the air. She started to laugh. Clint dropped her on the bed. "Yeehaw," he said and grinned at her. She grinned back, joy spreading through every inch of her. She felt so light and airy she was surprised that she wasn't floating above the bed. Clint took off his hat and his jacket, then lowered himself on top of her.

Laura wrapped her arms around his shoulder and pulled him tight against her. She felt so good and right wrapped up tight in Clint's body. She kissed him, her mouth yearning against his and he answered back with equal need until she lost track of time—of herself, of where she ended and Clint began.

"Woman, you're trying to kill me."

She nuzzled his neck. "If they saw this back at the station house they'd be shocked."

"The men would be jealous," Clint said. "About today. At the precinct. I wanted to tell you—"

"It's not important," Laura said and pulled his mouth back over hers. And it was true, none of the rest of the world was important...only the two of them together on her bed. She rolled over him and began to unbutton his shirt, letting her lips explore the inches of exposed skin.

Clint moaned. "Laura, it is important. They have the wrong image of you."

Laura sat astride him and pushed her pelvis against his very evident desire for her. She did not want to talk about their fellow officers. She wanted to lose herself in the madness of loving Clint. "They have the image of me that I want them to have. I don't care if a few of them laugh at me."

"Yes, you do. You're not as tough as you make out, Laura Carter—" Clint gasped as Laura's hands lowered the zipper of his jeans and stroked his erection.

She smiled. "Let's not talk."

Clint pushed himself against her as she explored the hot length of him. "Agreed," he rasped out, "no more talking about work tonight."

Laura found herself on her back and Clint's hand trailing up her thigh, pushing her nightgown higher, then his fingers were exploring between her legs and she thought she might explode right then.

"I can't wait," he said and pushed himself into her.

His gray eyes held her, compelled her with some unspoken emotion as he pushed himself into her body. She bit her lower lip to stop from shouting out at the pleasure; the need to have him. She closed her eyes against the emotions she was seeing in his face and the feelings she was afraid were shining from her eyes.

Clint began to stroke in and out of her and she rose to meet him. His hand captured her face turning her face back toward him. "Open your eyes, I want to see you," he demanded.

He kept his eyes locked on hers as their bodies mated,

faster and faster. "I—" she wanted to tell him something, but couldn't remember what as their bodies strained for the edge together.

"Laura," he cried out as he reached the crest and emptied himself inside her; she peaked as well...still looking into his eyes.

LAURA RAISED her head and kissed Clint on the chest, on his neck and then on his lips. "Good morning."

"Morning." Clint smiled and she felt like she could face anything today. He wrapped his arms around her and she snuggled against him. She wished they could stay in her bed forever.

"That was some night, cowboy."

"Only the best for a princess."

"I'm glad you're a man who knows how to treat a princess right." She sat up and grabbed her robe. "I'll go see if I have anything edible in the kitchen."

"Um, maybe that should wait until I tell you what I was going to say last night."

"Oh," she didn't like the way he sounded. She kneeled on the bed, "If you're going to tell me that you're going back home to Three Cow Weighing Station, then I don't want to hear it."

"Two Horse Junction. And yes, one of the messages waiting for me was from the sheriff. His doctor told him he has some mild heart problems so he's decided to retire early. I'm going back as soon as I can tie up all the loose ends here."

"But what about the promotion?"

"It doesn't really matter so much now. I'm going home."

"Oh." The word came out very softly. She felt cold and

empty. She traced a pattern along her chenille bedspread. "Oh," she repeated. "So this was goodbye."

Clint sat up and took her hand. "There's something I need to say."

His eyes searched hers for something. She knew he'd see sadness at the fact that he was leaving. She dropped her gaze and picked at a loose thread from her comforter. "I'm going to miss you. I kind of liked having our very own cowboy around the station house."

"I'm going to miss you, too."

"Maybe I could come and visit you sometime." The words were out of her mouth before she could stop them. She was sounding like a desperate female, unwilling to let go of what was no more than a one-night stand. Two-night stand. "I've never been to Texas," she added to justify why she might visit him.

"I don't think you should come," he said and Laura thought her heart might break. "You wouldn't like my town. And well, I'd rather remember you here." He reached out and stroked her face. "We both know we're completely wrong for each other. We're very different. We want different things out of life."

"You've got a list of candidates for the perfect wife waiting for you in Texas," she said.

He sighed. "I need to marry someone who wants the same things I do." He was silent and she couldn't think of anything to say. "You've already made the mistake of trying to make yourself fit into a man's life." He stroked her hair. "We both deserve to be happy."

She watched him get out of bed and get dressed, running arguments through her head as to why he was wrong about her not liking Two Horse. She could at least give it a chance.

She stopped, realizing she was doing it once again. She

was ready to throw away everything she had worked so hard for in order to follow a handsome cowboy home.

Clint put on his hat and faced her. "I'm going home in two weeks."

Laura hugged the pillow to herself. "What was it you wanted to say to me?"

He searched her face again, but she didn't know what he wanted to find there. "I wanted to tell you that I had a really good time. I like everything about you, Laura Carter. Even the princess routine." He grinned at her and walked to her bedroom door while Laura felt herself grow colder and colder.

This was the smart thing to do, she reminded herself. She and Clint could never have anything more than an affair. Clint put a hand on her doorframe and stopped with his back still to her, as if debating with himself.

Laura held her breath as he turned around. "Before, what I wanted to tell you is...I love you."

12

I LOVE YOU. Over the next month Laura heard those words over and over again in her head. They taunted her. The first thing she thought in the morning, the words she re-played as she went to sleep.

I love you.

If Clint loved her so much why had he left? Did he ex-pect her to go chasing after him to Five Jackass Place? Did he expect her to completely change her life and try to fit into his?

The morning he had made his shocking declaration she had stared at him openmouthed, unsure if she had heard him properly. He'd looked at her with a rueful smile tug-ging one corner of his mouth. *I love you.* What was she supposed to say to him?

"Don't worry, you don't have to say anything. My mama always raised her sons to tell the truth. And don't think I don't appreciate the irony of me falling for you. I was your toughest critic in our department."

"I wanted to sleep with you," she blurted out. "From the first day I met you, I...I thought about you a lot."

"You fancied me from the first day?" His gray eyes lightened. "I never knew that. So the old Marshall charm still works."

"You didn't like me." She hoped she wasn't pouting. She felt like pouting. She never pouted. She was definitely pouting.

"No, I didn't. You didn't like me, either. You just wanted me."

"Yes," she admitted.

"I won't bother you again," he said.

"You're not a bother," she answered. "We could continue to see each other...."

"For the next two weeks? If there's one thing we share it's the fact that neither of us are the kind of people who have flings."

I could have a fling with you, she wanted to shout. For Clint she was willing to break all her rules.

Clint walked back to her with long slow steps. He leaned over her and kissed her on the forehead. "I liked meeting you, Carter."

With those words he had left her. Left her life. He had remained in Chicago for another two weeks and then he had gone home.

She had to face the fact that she didn't attract men who had staying power. Her father. All of her mother's husbands. Brian and Joe. Funny how in comparison none of them mattered nearly as much as Clint.

He hadn't even asked her to go with him. Of course the idea of her living in a place like Three Cow Stop was ridiculous. There would be nothing for her to do, except be Mrs. Clint Marshall.

No matter how appealing that was in some ways, she couldn't lose her own identity, everything she worked to be. Quite simply, she wasn't the wife type. What she was was a cop, a good one.

Clint had said he loved her, and when she had remained frozen, unable to figure out what to say, he had kissed her gently on the forehead and left. Just like that. Loved her and left her.

If he loved her he would have stayed around. His career

wasn't more important than hers. Plus she didn't even love him.

She thought about him all the time, but that was because she was infatuated. She would get over it soon. She looked at the report she'd been filling out and wondered what Clint was doing. Probably arresting someone for tipping cows.

Did kids really tip cows or was that a rural myth that she, the ultimate of city girls, knew nothing about? Why, if she walked down the main street of One Limping Donkey Stop, the smallest child could tell her the most outrageous rural tale and she would have to believe them.

She would be a fish out of water. A city girl scraping manure off her stilettos. No, it couldn't be done.

After work, she'd stopped by Amber's apartment to visit with little Petey. Garrow had found Amber a clerical position in SFI. Somehow Garrow had made it very clear to Amber's former pimp that she was to be left alone and Amber hadn't had any more problems with him. She had enrolled in a night-school computer class, and Laura had baby-sat several evenings for her.

She'd also learned that Garrow was obsessed with the Monroe case because he'd seen it as his make-it-or-break-it case. If he brought in Monroe he was sure he would be fast-tracked. He'd laughed as he told Laura while playing with little Petey. "You'll understand my ambitions," he'd said to her. "I studied your records. We're a lot alike. Or at least, we used to be alike. It's funny but the more time I spend with this little guy, and Amber," he turned a little red when he said Amber's name, "I seem to be mellowing."

The case against Cassandra Monroe was proceeding well. Or as well as a few SFI agents combing the Monroe books again versus Cassandra's team of lawyers and forensic accountants. Garrow said it was going to take time, but in the end Cassandra would be spending a lot of time behind bars. Luckily Tom Watson was talking as fast as his lawyer could negotiate a better deal for his client.

Garrow thought he might be able to indict Nicholas Vasili as well.

The sound of her telephone ringing startled her back to reality. "Detective Carter."

"Laura is that you?"

"Mother. Is something wrong? Uncle Alfred, is he sick?"

"No, dear. Don't jump to conclusions, it's so common," her mother said exasperated. "I'm simply calling because I wanted you to come for dinner."

"Are you sure there's nothing wrong? You've never called me at work before."

There were a few seconds of silence before her mother cleared her throat. "Well, yes. I figured you would be so busy with your job, that you wouldn't want me disturbing you."

"Why do you want me to come to dinner?" Laura thought about the flight schedule to Boston. "I could catch a plane later tonight."

"Good heavens, dear, you're being silly. I told you there is no emergency. I simply want you to come for dinner on Saturday. I thought it would be nice to talk. I haven't seen you in ages."

"All right, I'll come on Saturday," Laura agreed wondering what the heck was going on. She and her mother often went for weeks without talking and months without seeing each other. They liked it that way.

"We can have a nice chat," her mother said again.

Was that a threat, Laura wondered as she hung up the phone.

The captain stuck his head out of his office. "Carter, get in here."

She wiped her suddenly sweaty hands on her pant legs and stood. The captain was looking through a file as she came in. She stood and waited. He closed the file. "Sit down." He moved his glass of green stuff to the side and took a file that had been under the glass. He took a swig of his drink. "After a while you get used to the stuff. Amazing what you'll do for love."

"Your wife is lucky to have such a committed man."

"Got married, lost twenty-five pounds and lowered my blood pressure. Funny thing is that when I first met my wife I didn't think it would work. We were set up on a blind date. I only asked her out a second time to be polite, then she had tickets to a hockey game so we went out again. Something clicked on that third date. I basically never left her again."

"Yes, sir," she said, wondering where he was going.

"Like you and Marshall. Never thought the two of you would click, but there you go."

What had Clint said? Had he shared stories about their affair with the guys over a beer? "Yes, sir," she said coldly.

"He said you were the best partner he'd ever had. Said I should recommend you for the homicide job."

"He did what?"

"That was before he knew he was leaving. Said you were more committed than any other cop he knew. So I'm taking it into account. I wanted to tell you that I put a letter of recommendation into your file."

"Thank you, sir. Does that mean..."

"That you got the promotion? Hell no. You need more experience before you can transfer over to homicide, but keep it up and you'll make it." Clark closed her file and studied her. "I gotta say I wasn't very happy when I was forced to take you into my department. I don't like being told what to do."

"I never meant—"

Clark raised his hand and Laura closed her mouth. At the very least she knew her boss didn't like to be interrupted. "As I was saying, I wasn't pleased at having you here. But you've done good work on all your cases, especially this Monroe investigation. I'm a big enough man to appreciate a good officer even if I didn't hire you. I'm glad you're on my team." He held his hand out to her and they shook. "Dismissed."

"Thank you, sir." She left Clark's office wondering if her whole world was shifting on its axis. At her desk she finished her reports wondering what Clint was doing now. As the shift drew to an end, Bill Horton, one of the more seasoned officers came up to her. "Some of us are going out for a beer. Want to come?"

Suddenly she was one of the guys.

"HELLO, MOTHER."

Her mother's cheek brushed her own. "You look very pale. And your hair. Really dear, if you'd only told me I would have made an appointment at Ricardo's."

"I'm only here for the evening."

"It wouldn't have taken long, you could have come in earlier this afternoon. You could look so nice if you only tried."

Laura pressed her palms together so she wouldn't jump out of her chair and strangle her mother. "I don't need to look like a debutante in my job."

"Surely it wouldn't hurt your career if you were well groomed."

"It makes absolutely no difference to my career if my hair...did you just say career?"

Veronica Ashworth patted her own hair, as if checking to see if one strand of her well-lacquered hair dared escape her French twist. "Why, yes, dear. There's no need to get so excited. George, you remember him, used to get excited over the most ridiculous things. Well, it was just so common. It was one of the main reasons we got divorced. I understand being a policewoman is important to you but I'd hate to see you begin to talk like they do on that blue movie."

"A dirty movie?" Laura was wondering if she'd somehow gone to the wrong address. Perhaps there was a series of Boston town homes filled with antiques and rich society divorcées who were never happy about their daughters.

"Yes, that N.Y. blue police force squad room something."

"*N.Y.P.D. Blue.* You mean *N.Y.P.D. Blue.*" Laura looked around the room. It was still her mother's favorite sitting room decorated in rose and cream. As a child she'd called it the Queen's tearoom because it was where her mother and her friends held court, gossiping over tea. It looked the same but her mother was behaving very oddly. "What did you mean about my being a police officer being important?"

Her mother picked up her drink and saw that it was empty. "Do you want a predinner cocktail? Where's Martha?" The maid, who had been standing in a corner, stepped forward. "Oh, there you are. I never know where you'll be hiding next. I'll have a martini," Veronica turned her sharp blue eyes on her daughter, "Darling, what do you want?"

"Soda water is fine."

"You heard us, Martha." Veronica Ashworth waited as Martha left the room. "Do you prefer police officer to policewoman? I'll have to remember that."

"Mother, what's making you talk like this?"

"Good heavens, dear, I don't know what you're going on about. I've always been very supportive of your choices."

Laura choked as a breath of air went down the wrong way. She stared at the woman aliens had left behind when they had abducted her mother. "Did you hit your head or something? Has Dr. Harvey seen you recently?"

"Laura, stop being so ridiculous."

"Maybe you've mixed up your medications. I can call Dr. Harvey and give him a complete list of your prescriptions." She narrowed her eyes. "You're not taking anything illegal are you?"

"For heaven's sake sit down. That young man of yours said you took all of this very seriously, but I'd never realized how accurate he was."

"What young man of mine?"

"The good looking muscular one. My, but he was handsome. And that Texas accent." Veronica played with the long strands of her pearl necklace, staring off into a distant memory. "I must say, if I wasn't your mother and if I was twenty years younger I would be more than willing to make him husband number six. For once I have to compliment you on your taste."

"Clint? Clint Marshall came to see you?"

"Yes, dear. I just told you that. He came about three weeks ago."

Laura frowned. Three weeks ago he had gone back to Texas. He'd left her life and it had never been going better. Captain Clark thought she was doing good work. Some of the other police officers were accepting her and the rumors about her were dying down. And Sweetums was barking away like a yappy little dog should.

Everything about her life, in fact, was perfect. She had everything she'd ever wanted: respect, friends and a dog. Perfect. Goddamn perfect.

And now her mother was actually talking to her about her job. Next she'd be asking her about her dreams and goals, asking her if she was happy.

"Are you happy, dear?"

"What?"

"That nice man, he said what you were doing made you happy. That sometimes I made you unhappy." Her mother blinked. "Really, when I asked your Uncle Alfred to try to get you to change your mind about that nasty job, I never meant to hurt you."

"Mother, I know that but—"

"Well that's all in the past, no point in rehashing it now. The important thing is for us to move forward. It was so nice of you to come for dinner. I asked Uncle Alfred to come as well. He was saying how much he missed seeing you."

Her mother looked away from her. "Ah, here's Martha with our drinks. Are you sure you don't want anything a little stronger in your glass? No, well suit yourself."

"Mother."

"I always meant well, dear." Her mother sighed and took another sip of her drink.

"You've always been a proper daughter. The truth is that I thought you'd get over this silly rebellious need to have a career. The need to leave me. We've always been together, the two of us. I never believed you'd move so far away."

"I told you how important being a police officer was. I

need to be something other than the daughter of a wealthy family."

"What's wrong with being my daughter?"

"Nothing. I'm happy to be your daughter," Laura said and realized she meant it. "But I want to have something that is mine."

"Well, yes, Mr. Marshall explained that to me. I must say, Laura, if you had only been clear I would never have interfered. But he told me how well you were doing in Chicago."

Her mother continued to nervously play with her pearls. "I wish I had understood all of this before. Then you could have been doing this in Boston instead of in that awful city."

Laura stared at her mother in amazement. With one conversation Clint had managed to explain her feelings to this woman who had never listened to a word she'd said? How was that possible?

Or had she too easily accepted her mother's lack of support? Maybe she had never tried hard enough to tell her mother why she'd wanted to be something more than a Carter of the Boston Carters.

Had she tried hard enough with Clint? Was there more she could have done? Told him how she felt about him. Asked him to stay?

But Clint wanted to be home with the family and friends he had left behind. From the way he had described Two Horse Junction, his love for the people and the land, she understood why he wanted to go home. Because it was *home*. She looked around the room of the mansion her mother lived in. It had been part of their family for years, but she had never felt at home in it.

Uncle Alfred entered the room, casting a nervous look at her, and she realized that he too, was regretting his actions. She set down her tea cup, stood up and, to his shock, hugged him.

People were what made up her home, she finally understood.

13

CLINT SIGNED the payroll sheet, raised his head and surveyed his domain. Through the front window of his office he could see Main Street. Lilly Sinclair walked into the grocers as Mrs. Winchell came out. They exchanged a few pleasantries and Mrs. Winchell started down the street stopping in front of Rosie's dress shop. The striking redhaired retired school teacher waved at someone inside the shop and then continued her afternoon stroll. Every afternoon Mrs. Winchell walked the exact same route to her friend Mrs. Betty Jane Perkins's house for tea and gossip. In the month that he'd been home, he'd joined the ladies for tea twice and learned more about what had occurred in Two Horse Junction while he was away than all the stories his brothers, Bernard and Dylan, his mother and the deputy sheriff had told him combined.

Once Mrs. Winchell had stepped into Rosie's dress shop, Main Street became empty of people. He kept looking but other than the sun shining off the window of Rosie's, nothing moved or changed on the street.

He leaned back on his chair and sighed with satisfaction. This was what he wanted. Life in a small town. Soon the school would let out and the kids would race down to the grocery store to buy candy or soda and hang out on the store's stoop. That was the signal for him to take a walk around town. His assistant deputy would finish his lunch break soon and take over the early evening shift.

Clint would be on call for the rest of the night but his cell phone hadn't rung once since he'd come home.

After he finished his shift he'd head over to his mother's for dinner. Once a week she liked to have all her boys eat a home-cooked meal together. He grinned. Yup, this was what he wanted to be doing, spending time with his family, getting to know everyone in town and keeping the peace in Two Horse Junction. Life just didn't get any better than this. Until he got married and started his own family that is.

His gaze fell to the papers on the desk and they practically screamed traitor at him. He shoved them into a manila folder and pushed the folder to the corner of his desk. After dinner he would sit outside on his front porch, stare at the stars of the Texas sky and decide what to do about the papers.

He wondered what Laura was doing.

The manila folder taunted him from the corner of the desk. Later. He'd decide later.

The door to the sheriff's office opened and a tall, dark-haired man who looked an awful lot like Clint entered. "Hey, Sheriff Marshall." For some reason of his own peculiar sense of humor, Ben loved calling his brother Sheriff Marshall. Ben was the quintessential Texas cowboy—strong and silent. He kept most of his thoughts to himself, and while Clint was sure that most of the time he was thinking about his horses, sometimes Ben seemed to have his own private jokes about everyone in Two Horse.

"Caught any nefarious criminals today?"

"Ben."

His brother grinned at him and pushed back his hat as he straddled a chair. "Mom wanted me to remind you to bring a bouquet of flowers tonight."

"Why does Mom want a bouquet? She has a garden filled with flowers."

Ben looked at his brother and his lips definitely twitched. "Not for her. They're for Betty Perkins."

"Mrs. Perkins is coming to dinner?" Clint preferred the evening when dinner was only family. "Is Mrs. Winchell coming as well? We won't get a word in edgewise with mom and those two chattering away about everyone who's ever lived or passed through town."

"Not old Mrs. Perkins. Her daughter. Betty. Mom invited her to dinner so you could meet her. She's the latest candidate on Mom's list of women suitable to marry Clint. I've gotta tell you, she's beautiful. Mom's concerned that she's only visiting her mother, Betty lives in California now, but Mom thinks you can sweep her off her feet and convince her to live in her old hometown. Now that you've suddenly gotten so fussy Mom's got her hands full trying to find the right woman for you." Ben smiled like the cat that had eaten the canary and still had a feather sticking out of its mouth. "From your earlier letters to Mom when you went on and on about how much you wanted to come home and start your real life, I thought you would be engaged by now. Don't look so surprised. Of course Mom read your letters to us. Anything to keep Dylan in town."

Clint sighed. "I've only been home for a month. You don't decide on the woman you want to spend the rest of your life with that quickly." Except he'd fallen in love with Laura in less than a week. Unfortunately it was taking him longer to fall out of love with her.

That was the problem with the Marshalls. Love stuck to them. His mother loved his father despite how often he'd betrayed her. Sometimes he thought that Ben still loved the woman who had divorced him after only two months of marriage. Why did the Marshalls only fall in love with people who didn't have staying power? His eyes fell on the manila folder again. Maybe he already knew the answer. He had to find out....

"A month is plenty enough time according to Mom. She wants to know why you've been dragging your feet. In fact the whole town does. Don't tell me some cute Chicago gal caught your heart?"

Clint met his brother's far too piercing gaze calmly. He hadn't told anyone about Laura and he wasn't about to until he'd decided. At first, it had been because he had considered Laura part of his past—of his life before he became sheriff of Two Horse Junction. And now it was just ornery pride; he didn't want to admit that being back home was not everything he'd dreamed it would be.

"I came back home to start my life," Clint answered, aware that he could still do that. If he forgot all about Laura.

"I know. But you didn't have to come home to take care of us."

He looked at his younger brother sharply. What did Ben mean? He knew full well that his brothers were grown men. He came home because he wanted to. "I came home because I wanted to live here."

"Good, because sometimes I wonder if you really know why you came back. When we were growing up you were so determined to make up for all of Dad's mistakes."

"Dad was an asshole."

"Yes, I know. We all know, even Mom. We don't have anything left to prove in this town. People respect us, like us for who we are. They like us. Well at least they like me. Dylan they find puzzling."

"And me. They like me."

"Driven. You're very driven. Determined. You have a

plan." His brother settled his long frame more comfortably on the chair, looking like he was set to spend the afternoon.

"My plan was to come back home." Clint said crossly. Didn't Ben have a ranch he should be managing? "I wanted to come back to Two Horse. It's home."

"First you had to make a success of yourself away from here. So that everyone in Two Horse would know that you deserved to be sheriff. The only problem with your plan is that you were the only one who had any doubts about yourself. Everyone else in town always knew you would be a great sheriff. I hope that you know it, too. I hope you proved it to yourself." Ben stood up. "Don't forget the flowers." With his last words Ben laughed and walked out the door.

What the heck was Ben finding so funny?

Clint watched him turn up Main Street, and wondered briefly who else Ben was visiting in town before he went back to his ranch. His brother had acquired a big spread and spent most of his days working the land. Unlike Clint or Dylan, Ben had never left town. As a child he'd spent all his time at their uncle Jackson's ranch, and to no one's surprise he'd inherited the ranch when Jackson had died of cancer five years ago. Clint had been away for much of the time so he'd missed his uncle's long and painful demise. His mother had nursed her brother throughout his illness and Ben had taken care of the ranch.

Clint thought of the dinner ahead of him tonight at his mother's house. So far his mother had invited Charlotte, a school teacher, Lucy, a rancher, Andrea, the bank manager and now Betty Perkins to dinner. He'd mildly enjoyed the dinners and taken each of the women out, but despite the fact that Charlotte was beautiful, that he and

Lucy shared a love of horses, that he and Andrea had both lived in Dallas, he had not been interested.

The folder on his desk stared back at him. Did he dare? What if he made the biggest mistake of his life? What if he didn't? He grabbed the papers, walked over to the fax and punched in the numbers. With a curious feeling of time suspended and simultaneously having his universe turning upside down he pressed the send button and watched the papers begin to make their way through the machine.

There. He was committed. Right or wrong, he was about to try.

The door to the office burst open and his other brother, Dylan, rushed in. Blond and exceedingly handsome, he looked very unlike his fraternal twin, Ben. Dylan looked like their father. "You have to come to Lilly's."

"Has she redecorated the front parlor again?" Dylan spent an inordinate amount of time at Lilly's, listening to her plans for the hotel and for Two Horse Junction.

"There's a fine city gal sitting on her front stoop talking to Lilly and her cohorts about the Texas cowboy who broke her heart. Seduced her and abandoned her, was how she described him."

Inside Clint sighed, but he kept his expression impassive. He didn't understand Dylan and his fondness for the town's gossip. He picked up a pencil and began to oversee the payroll report. "I don't have time for your crazy stories. If Lilly has a new eccentric guest I'm bound to meet her soon enough. Mother will undoubtedly invite her to dinner next week. I'll hear all about the man who abandoned her then." He realized he'd snapped the pencil in two. "Lilly should change the sign of her hotel to Heartbreak Hotel."

Dylan laughed and perched on the side of Clint's desk. "Lilly's not that bad. She just likes to surround herself with personalities. Trust me, the last thing she would ever consider herself is a romantic counselor. If you knew what she'd...Never mind." He tried to look at the pages going through the fax machine but Clint grabbed them and stuffed them back into their manila folder. "What were you sending?"

"Just some papers that the Chicago department needed."

"I thought you were finished with your Chicago job. You've hardly even talked about it. I have to admit I thought that something rather untoward might have happened. Did it?"

"No."

"Of course not. Big brother Clint would never do anything that breaks the rules." Dylan sat down in the chair his brother has vacated, but unlike his twin he didn't straddle his chair. Instead he sat and crossed his legs, the crease on his khaki pants crisp. "Is being back home everything you thought it would be?"

"It takes a while to settle in." Clint wondered why his brothers had chosen today to begin questioning his life.

"You do know that Ben and I are fully grown now. We don't need you to look after us anymore."

"I came back home because I want to be here." Clint wondered why he was having to clarify his reasoning to his family.

"That's good, because it's nice to have you. Mom will like having you around when I'm gone."

"You're leaving?" Ben had been hinting about this earlier. Why didn't he know anything about his brother's plans?

"With you home to look after Mother and Ben taking care of the ranch, it seems like a good time to make a break. See what else might be out there."

"What do you want to do?"

"I've got some ideas, but nothing definite yet. I'm not about to uproot all my stakes. Not like that pretty Boston gal at Lilly's."

"Boston?" Clint turned his attention away from the payroll spreadsheet to his brother. "She's from Boston?"

"From one of their most established families she told Lilly."

It couldn't be.

He felt the blood rush away from his head as his body reacted to the idea of Laura being here. In Two Horse Junction. His heart pounded hard in his own ears and he had difficulty focusing on his brother.

"Why is she here?" he demanded in a harsh voice.

"She's here to find the cowboy who broke her heart."

Clint stood and his chair fell back. "What's her name?"

Dylan flashed his lady-killer smile that reminded Clint of their father. "Laura. Her name is Laura."

"Laura Carter?"

Dylan raised an eyebrow. "She didn't give her family name. She said the cowboy who broke her heart would know who she was."

"Is she beautiful?"

"Most women are."

"Blond?"

Dylan nodded.

"Around five-nine? With a tiny fluffball dog?"

"Calling a Lhasa apso a dog is rather an insult to the breed. She is a pedigree," Dylan argued agreeably.

But Clint was already out the door. In front of Rosie's Mrs. Winchell, carrying a hatbox, stepped outside the shop into his path, forcing him to stop. He tipped his hat. "Mrs. Winchell."

She nodded. "My, you're in a hurry. You almost

knocked me over." She scanned him from head to toe. "I understand Betty Perkins is having dinner with your family tonight."

"Yes, ma'am." His feet itched to keep going, but good manners kept him in place.

"It's nice that you're meeting the young ladies in town, but Betty isn't the one for you." She narrowed her eyes as she studied his face. "Is something wrong?" She shook her head at her own foolishness. "My, I must say I never noticed how much there was of your father in you."

"Ma'am?"

"Oh, I know you're not happy being reminded of him, but there's something of him in your eyes. And probably something in your desire to prove yourself elsewhere." She moved her purse from one hand to the other. "It's not my place to say, but that's never stopped me before. The habits of a school teacher, retired or not, are too hard to break. It's too bad your father never had his chance to sow his wild oats before he fell in love with your mother."

Why did everyone want to talk about his father today? Clint tried edging around Mrs. Winchell, he needed to get to Lilly's before his racing heart gave him a heart attack. "There's little my father could have done to excuse his actions. I believe he stole from your family as well."

"Yes, I lost money when your father left town for good." She snorted. "Serves me right for being fooled by a charmer. And he was *some* charmer. Not that I think you're like that. You are what he wanted to be. I'm sorry if I'm upsetting you. I just wanted to let you know that we, my family, have never held a grudge against your family or your mother because of your father. We were all taken by him. We all liked him. But he didn't have your substance. Now I can see I'm keeping you from some official duty I'm sure. Go ahead. I'll see you at the church picnic on Sunday."

Clint escaped Mrs. Winchell and had made it halfway to Lilly's hotel when Lou Barnett stepped outside his barber shop. Following the dictates of small-town life, Clint slowed to smile at the man. "Barnett," he said, hoping the man didn't want to have a conversation.

"Hear there's a stranger in town."

Clint nodded.

"Glad you're going to check her out for yourself. What a story she's telling about one of us charming her and then breaking her heart. I know everyone in Two Horse will be glad to hear that you're gonna fix her problem."

"Er, yes. I thought I should check out the situation."

"We've missed you over the years. Your mother especially. She was looking forward to the day you came back and started making babies."

"I was hoping to get married first."

"That goes without saying. Why even your father had the decency to get married. Too bad it never stuck with him. Not so sure if your brother is going to stay."

"Dylan?"

"It'll be interesting. What do you suppose that gal wants?" He leaned in conspiratorially, wanting to have information to share with his customers tomorrow. "Do you think she's some kind of big city con artist?"

"I think you've been renting too many movies from The Feed Store."

Barnett chuckled. "I love those thrillers with beautiful women who are dangerous to love. Yup. I hear the gal is real pretty. A real fashion plate all dressed in pink and a pink bow on her dog." Barnett started to sweep the steps in front of his shop. "Yup, it sure does sound like something. You'd best head on over to Lilly's."

Clint hurried toward the hotel, passing a pair of teen-agers and Dorothy Harnell. "Sorry Sheriff, can't talk to-day. My hair appointment went late," she said as she passed him. Which meant she'd heard the pretty stranger's tale at Lilly's and was rushing home to start spreading the news.

Everyone in Two Horse was about to know about Laura before he did!

Finally he was in front of the hotel and saw a group of Lilly's regulars laughing and talking on the front veranda. "The man never stopped talking about Two Horse Junction and its wonderful people, all five hundred and eighty-seven of you. He planned to increase the population as soon as he found the right kind of woman to marry and get her in the family way," Clint heard a familiar voice say. "His mother has a list of appropriate women for him to marry."

"But why didn't he want to marry you?" Miss Sheila Kelly asked. "You seem very nice. I like your dog and you dress with real class. I would think he should have been happy to marry you."

"My dog is a real hero," Laura said as Clint pushed his way through the crowd. His breath caught in his throat at the sight of her sitting on the porch swing wearing a short pink dress with Sweetums, including the matching pink bow, drooling on her lap. Laura had placed a lace hand-kerchief underneath the fluffball's mouth to catch the ex-cess slobber. Clint was behind her, so she didn't see him, but Sweetums stirred and sniffed the air.

Laura paused dramatically. "He thought I was all wrong for Texas. He said that Boston and Texas didn't match, but he wasn't giving me any credit. I can fit in any-where."

Sheila tsked. "That boy has a stubborn streak a mile

long. He was always damned and determined to show that he was different from his daddy." The group around Laura nodded in agreement with Sheila.

So all of Two Horse thought he was stubborn and obsessed with repairing his father's reputation. What else did they say behind his back?

"Did you really have a five day affair with him and then he just abandoned you?" Lilly wanted to know. She smiled at Clint, enjoying the show that was about to unfold.

"We were together for five days, but we only were *together*, if you catch my drift, for two nights." Laura leaned in confidentially. "Only slightly better than a one-night stand I'm afraid. I was never that kind of girl. My mother raised me better."

Sweetums stood on her paws and tried to look behind Laura. She barked loud and strong for such a small dog. Laura patted Sweetums head. "It's all right, dear. There aren't any wolves in this very nice hotel."

Clint bared his teeth as he moved forward. "I wouldn't be so sure of that." He stopped in front of Laura, the ladies surrounding her dispersing like a herd of sheep that had indeed found a wolf in their midst.

Laura stood. "Sheriff Marshall. How nice to see you. I was just telling these very nice ladies about you."

"What are you doing here?" Clint concentrated on keeping his arms by his side and not throttling her. From the little he had heard, Laura had told the good ladies of Lilly's plenty. Too much! How did she expect him to live in this town with his reputation in shatters?

Laura put Sweetums on the ground and the dog raced the four steps to him, sat down on her hind legs and drooled on his cowboy boots. To give himself a moment to gather his shaken wits, he stooped down and patted her on the head. Sweetums expelled even more saliva and then, as if sensing it was best to make herself scarce, she found herself a nice shady spot under a chair and curled into a ball.

Lilly put her arm through Sheila's and motioned to the other women. "Ladies, I think we should leave Laura and her cowboy alone."

"I'm not her cowboy," Clint growled, annoyed by the women's knowing smirks. He was trying to quash down that part of him that was thrilled at seeing Laura, at the idea that she had decided to come to Two Horse Junction. But she had no idea what she was getting herself into. Look at her. She had pearls in her ears, flowers on her shoes and a silly dog with a bow.

Once they were alone, Laura smiled, her blue eyes shining with a warm light. Every part of his body grew hot and he concentrated on keeping his feet firmly planted on the front porch, keeping his distance from her.

"I was hoping you'd find me," she said.

"I am a police officer and you certainly made it very clear to everyone in town that you were here." He didn't want to ask her why she was here—not just yet. He liked looking at her. In his best Texas drawl, he said, "You're not dressed for Texas."

"I'm dressed like a Boston blue blood."

"You never dressed like that in Chicago."

"No. But you do seem to have a pretty specific impression of me. Of what I can and cannot do. You never asked me to come with you."

They were circling each other like a pair of gunfighters at high noon. "I was coming back here."

"I know. You made that very clear."

"Two Horse isn't for you."

"You said you loved me and then you never gave me a

chance." Laura's eyes glittered. "You said you loved me and then you just left. You never even let me think about the idea...of us."

Unable to resist any longer he reached out and tucked a strand of honey blond hair back into the complicated arrangement she wore on her head. "My mother tried being married to someone who was all wrong for her and for this town. It didn't work. My father was miserable here. My mother couldn't imagine living anywhere else."

"That was your mother and your father. Not us." She raised her chin and stared him down. "We have more in common than you want to admit. We know what it's like to have others judge us because of who they think we are."

"That's true," he agreed. "But you wouldn't like it here. There's nothing for you to do."

She touched the necklace around her neck and let her hand linger there. "I'll figure something out. I'm smart. The important thing is that I'll be with you."

"Happy." He laughed bitterly. "In Two Pony Pit Stop?" He shook his head and shoved his hands into his pockets so that he wouldn't reach out and grab her and pull her into his arms and kiss her. All he wanted to do was take her home and make love to her in his antique bed until she never thought about leaving Two Horse Junction. Until the morning came—whether it was in a week, a month or a year—she would wake up and realize that a small Texas town wasn't for her.

Laura continued to stare at him stubbornly. "I'll adjust."

"You've worked hard to be a successful police officer. I'm the sheriff of Two Horse. Considering the fact that I also have a full-time deputy, there's no job for you."

"Being a good cop was very important to me. I wanted

to be something very different from my family." She shrugged. "I can do something else."

He reached for her hand. "This is your pattern, remember? You fall for some guy and then change your life to suit his. I can't let you do that." He raised her hand to his mouth and brushed his lips across her knuckles, intoxicated by the scent and warmth of her. He wanted to keep holding on to her forever. Instead he dropped her hand.

"I missed you. But this isn't the place for you. Take a look around." He swept a hand down Main Street. "Look, that's all there is."

"I love you," she said.

He felt his breath catch in his throat. "I didn't know that. Before...you—"

"I was scared. When you said you loved me it scared me to death. I was afraid I was making the same mistake my mother did. The same mistake I made with my fiancé." She took a step away from him, put her arms on the porch railing and took a breath as she looked at Main Street. "But it's not the same at all. I'm not scared anymore." She smiled tremulously. "I had almost decided to come after you. I was working up my nerve and then my mother told me what you did for me. You actually made her understand me. Thank you."

She faced him, crossing her arms across her chest. "I never found the words I needed with her. You did. That's what made me understand how you were different from the other men in my life. The men I thought I cared for, but who always disappointed me. They weren't right for me." She took a breath. "You are. And that made me understand I shouldn't be scared of love."

But he realized she *was* scared. Her face had drained of color and her lips trembled as she waited for him to respond to her declaration.

"I was coming back to Chicago. I faxed my request for a reassignment a half hour ago," he admitted.

"You did? Why?" she demanded, her hands gripped tightly together.

"I was coming for you. Being back here was very nice, but I realized it wasn't home. Where we are together. That's home. I want us to be together. To get married."

"Yes." She said promptly.

"I don't remember asking...yet."

"I'm not missing my window of opportunity. Yes I will marry you and become Laura Marshall."

"I thought you didn't approve of women who took their husband's name." He stood inches away from her, the air between them crackling.

"I like your name. It will be easier for our children if we have the same name. Besides, in a small town, especially being married to the sheriff, I think it's kind of obligatory. I'm afraid they would talk about us."

"You can be sure the whole damn town is talking about us." He put his hands around her waist and raised her slightly so that her lips were an inch away from his. "How many babies do you want?"

"Shouldn't you kiss me before we decide how many children we have?"

"Once I start kissing you I'm not going to stop so I want to clear up all the particulars first. You're kind of ornery so I don't want you saying I seduced you and tricked you into agreeing to children under the allure of my cowboy charm."

"Cowboy charm! You are full of yourself, Clint Marshall." She wrapped her arms around his neck. "I want three kids."

"That's good. We can always decide on more if we want."

"Will you take me to meet your family?"

"We can go to my mother's house for dessert." After he had made love to her. Slaked his thirst for her briefly.

"Kiss me," she said.

"We'll live in Chicago," he said. "Unless you want to go back home to Boston."

She dropped her hands from around his neck and stomped her foot hard on his cowboy boot. He let go of her. "Ouch, that hurt woman."

"My home is with you. We'll stay here."

"No. We'll move back to Chicago."

Laura poked him the chest. "You are the most stubborn, irritating man a woman ever had the good fortune to fall in love with."

He grabbed her hand and pulled her against his chest. His pulse raced as he looked down at her flushed face, her blue eyes burning with emotion. Once he'd thought she was cold? He couldn't imagine it. "Damn it, woman, I'm going to take you to bed. We'll settle this argument later."

Laura's breath caught and then she smiled at him. "Please, let's try living here. After all, I've done something I never would have imagined, I've fallen in love with a cowboy. Give me a chance to fall in love with your town. If it doesn't work—but it will—" she added passionately, "we'll find some other place. I fell in love with the first Texan I met, give me a chance to fall in love with the whole darn state."

How in the world had he been so lucky as to get this woman? "You got a deal, Princess. As long as you don't fall in love with any other cowboys. I'm gonna die if I don't kiss you."

"Then kiss me, cowboy."

Finally Clint pressed his mouth over hers and knew he was home. A long time later, after a thorough round of applause from Lilly and her ladies, they came up for air. Laura's face was almost as pink as her dress, but her blue eyes shone at him.

"Come on," he said as he grabbed her hand and pulled her along the porch to where Sweetums was dozing under a chair. He scooped the dog into one arm.

Laura stopped. "Where are you taking me?"

"To bed."

"Oh." Her face turned even pinker. "You can't just announce that you're taking me to bed on Main Street so that everyone in Three Dog Intersection knows. For heaven's sake, it's not proper!"

"Two Horse Junction. And it's the Texas way."

Clint took a step toward her and Laura raised her chin. Her mouth twitched. "Don't you dare."

"A cowboy never backs down from a dare." Clint grinned back at her and threw her over his shoulder. Cradling Sweetums against his chest and the love of his life over his shoulder he walked down Main Street toward his house. Laura might have to meet his family tomorrow.

Lou Barnett came out of his barber shop his mouth hanging open. "Evenin', Lou." Clint tipped his hat.

He felt Laura wiggling. "Stop that, what are you doing?"

"I'm waving to the ladies from Lilly's, and that nice man who's rubbing his eyes like he can't believe what he's seeing."

"It's not every day we have a fine city gal like you visit."

"It's not every day my bum is stuck up in the air for all to see but it sure does seem to happen a lot when I'm around you." Laura started to laugh. "I think we're going to have a wonderful life together."

"Damn right."

"Is your house close by, because I have a real hankering to kiss you again."

"Very close. When did you pick up that Texas talk?" Clint opened the gate to his house.

"From you. I'm testing it out. Are we here? Is this your house?" Laura twisted around his body trying to see.

"Careful, I'm going to drop you."

"You'd never do that." He reached the front steps, Sweetums jumped out of his arms onto the porch and Clint let Laura slide down his body. She wrapped her arms around his neck and kissed him as she made her way down while he blindly searched for the doorknob to get them inside and away from all the prying eyes of Two Horse.

"I love you," she whispered as she licked his ear.

Finally he had the door open. A white bundle of fur raced past him into her new home. He was about to pull Laura inside when he turned around and looked at the group of people staring at him: his deputy, Lou Barnett, Lilly Sinclair, Sheila Kelly, Mrs. Winchell and others. He raised his hand which stopped their chatter. He clasped Laura's hand. "This is Ms. Laura Carter," he said in a voice loud enough for all of Texas to hear. "She's consented to be my bride." Applause broke out. "Now we haven't seen each other for over a month so we'd like some time alone."

"What's Laura got to say," Lilly shouted as Clint had been about to pull Laura into his home.

Laura smiled and tucked her arm around Clint's. "I'm deliriously happy and looking forward to meeting each and every person of my new hometown, Two Horse Junction. Tomorrow." She giggled. "But the one thing I have to say, at the risk of repeating myself." She paused and her eyes locked with Clint's.

"I can't believe I'm marrying the cowboy!"

Clint grinned with the complete happiness of a man deliriously in love and scooped her up and carried her over the threshold. "Only the very best for a princess."

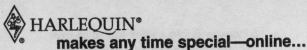

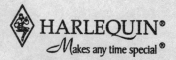